THE
IMAGINATION
BOX

THE IMAGINATION BOX

MARTYN FORD

Delacorte Press

Text copyright © 2015 by Martyn Ford
Jacket art copyright © 2016 by Steve Scott

All rights reserved. Published in the United States by Delacorte Press, an imprint of Random House Children's Books, a division of Penguin Random House LLC, New York. Originally published in paperback by Faber & Faber, London, in 2015.

Delacorte Press is a registered trademark and the colophon is a trademark of Penguin Random House LLC.

Visit us on the Web! randomhousekids.com

Educators and librarians, for a variety of teaching tools, visit us at RHTeachersLibrarians.com

Library of Congress Cataloging-in-Publication Data
Names: Ford, Martyn.
Title: The Imagination Box / Martyn Ford.
Description: First U.S. edition. | New York : Delacorte Press, [2016] | Originally published in the United Kingdom by Faber & Faber in 2015. | Summary: "A ten-year-old orphan discovers a box that can make the things he imagines become real and must keep the contraption from getting into the wrong hands with the help of a professor, his granddaughter, and a well-versed finger monkey"—Provided by publisher.
Identifiers: LCCN 2016008028 | ISBN 978-1-101-93627-6 (hardback) | ISBN 978-1-101-93629-0 (glb) | ISBN 978-1-101-93628-3 (ebook)
Subjects: | CYAC: Inventions—Fiction. | Imagination—Fiction. | Orphans—Fiction. | Adoption—Fiction. | Adventure and adventurers—Fiction. | BISAC: JUVENILE FICTION / Action & Adventure / General. | JUVENILE FICTION / Social Issues / Friendship. | JUVENILE FICTION / Family / Adoption.
Classification: LCC PZ7.1.F66 Im 2016 | DDC [Fic]—dc23
LC record available at http://lccn.loc.gov/2016008028

The text of this book is set in 12-point Bookman.
Interior design by Trish Parcell

Printed in the United States of America
10 9 8 7 6 5 4 3 2 1
First U.S. Edition

Random House Children's Books
supports the First Amendment and celebrates the right to read.

FOR INGE

PROLOGUE

"There is a box. Anything you imagine will appear inside. You have one go, one chance to create *anything* you want. What would you pick?"

The professor's voice echoed through the huge theater. He sipped his water, and took a deep breath. For him, this was a big moment.

The audience waited quietly, hundreds of men and women—a sea of faces. There were academics, members of the press, and select members of the public, all pondering the question. A cube-shaped object, about the size of a microwave, was on the desk next to the professor. Although a purple velvet sheet was hiding the item, every eye in the room drifted toward it. With another deep breath, he arranged his notes on the lectern in front of him, pressed the little button on his microphone, cleared his throat, and began to speak once more.

"Such a device, indeed, sounds impossible. . . ."

His nerves had calmed a little; he glanced down. His hands were almost steady. The professor then took the microphone from its stand and walked confidently across the stage to the desk.

"And yet, here we are," he said, "at the beginning. Ladies and gentlemen, it is with great pleasure that I present to you, on this humble stage, on this humble Saturday . . ." He whisked the sheet off his invention. The crowd watched on, silent now. . . .

CHAPTER 1

One month earlier . . .

The Dawn Star Hotel stood proud, even in the rain. A muggy storm swelled above the city. Tim was sitting in the hotel's huge, well-lit lobby, looking out at the flurry of rush-hour workers making their way home.

It was the first day of the first week of summer vacation. As usual, Tim was drawing. Hunched over a bird's-eye view of the umbrellas outside, he scribbled away. As he was a bit of a messy artist, his picture didn't *really* resemble the rainy street scene at all. But he knew what it was supposed to be, and surely that was what mattered.

"Don't you touch that sofa!" Elisa shrieked, rushing across the lobby.

She barreled toward Tim, as if his getting marks on the cushions were an emergency of giant proportions. After wetting her cloth with the bottle of spray she was clutching, she began firmly scrubbing Tim's hands. She huffed when she saw pencil smudges on his face. Tim frowned at the smell of the cloth as it scraped up and down his cheek. This wasn't the first time she had cleaned him in the same manner she cleaned any other object. In wide-eyed horror he watched a huge drip of soapy water splash onto his masterpiece. He slammed his sketch pad shut.

"I have told you more than once about sitting here," Elisa said.

"I was drawing the people outside."

"The consultant is arriving shortly. The last thing he'll want to see is you sitting in the lobby covered in pencil lead."

"I doubt that's the *last* thing he'll want to see," Tim muttered. Nonetheless, he gathered his pencils and stood to leave.

"And, Tim, don't touch the cakes in the function room. They're for the staff—Donald's called a meeting."

Tim headed out of the reception area, pushing his way through the broad oak doors into the long red-and-gold-carpeted hallway. Eyes fixed on the floor, he let his imagination get the better of him. In his mind, this wasn't a carpet at all; this was a river of lava, and the spirals were his stepping-stones. Walking on the lighter parts would, therefore, result in a grizzly death. So he hopped from rock to rock, past the ground-floor rooms, each with the same door but a different, ascending bronze number.

Hang on, what's this? Delicious smells from the function room at his side slowed his pace. Chocolate? Certainly. Strawberry sponge cake? Without a doubt. He stopped. Tasty, fresh, and, most appealing of all, forbidden cakes. How could he possibly resist such temptation?

But wait. Tim spotted Mary, the decidedly dumpling-shaped head chambermaid, at the supply closet, preparing to do her rounds, the slight whiff of bleach and fresh towels rising from her cart.

"Hello," he said. She just gave a big smile in return.

Mary didn't speak much English, but she could muster enough to rat him out to Elisa if the truth about this cakey mission ever came to light. So he waited patiently on his rock, like some kind of confectionary ninja, with glowing lava licking at his feet. Mary just trampled through the bubbling magma as if it weren't even there, pushing her cart along and round the corner, out of sight.

Above him, mounted on the wall near the ceiling, was a security camera, one of hundreds recently installed at the hotel. It gently turned its lens up and down the hall. Tim waited a moment, until it was facing away, and then approached the function room door.

This kind of heist was a fairly typical pastime. Living where he did, at the Dawn Star, Tim had to make his own fun. After all, not really having any friends his own age (that being ten, as of last month), he spent the vast majority of his time either alone or with adults. But that was fine; he had decided a long time ago that he preferred his own company anyway. Paper, pencil, and escaping into his own imagination—this is what Tim thought made him happy. It had never crossed his mind that he might need more.

The hotel had been Tim's home for nearly three years now, since his adoption. It sat in the center of Glassbridge, a quaint city full of history, complete with old buildings, wonky roofs, cobblestone streets, rusted iron railings, and statues of people on horseback. The place was to tourists what jam is to wasps, so the hotel was always full and the streets always busy.

Inside the function room, all the royal-red chairs were set out around a long, well-polished table. Still clutching his sketch pad under his arm and his pencils in his hand, Tim proceeded. There were some tables on the other side of the room, full of all kinds of food—platters of perfectly triangular sandwiches and, as expected, cake. There was also a display of the Dawn Star chocolate fudge puddings, individually presented in little glass bowls, complete with the hotel's logo on the side. Sadly, the layout was symmetrical, meaning one missing would be noticed. But then he spotted a tray of large chocolate brownies. Like playing a game of Jenga, he picked one up from the back of the pyramid and carefully removed it without disturbing the others. Still warm, he noticed. Excellent.

It was time to leave. He turned on his heel but stopped dead in his tracks, dropping his pad. The path was blocked by an old man wearing a pair of thick glasses, a rough lab coat over a white shirt, and a tie. Some kind of scientist, Tim thought. The sketch pad had fallen open on the floor; the man looked down at the umbrella picture, crouching to retrieve it.

"Indeed, yes, I could have done with one of those," he said, passing the pad back.

His lab coat was wet, his shoulders peppered with raindrops. He had curled wisps of gray hair bursting from the sides of his head, and his gold-framed glasses had those little half-moon magnifiers in the bottom for reading.

Tim took the pad with his free hand, without uttering a word.

"They *are* umbrellas, aren't they?" the man asked. "In your drawing?"

"Yes, they are," Tim replied.

As he rarely drew things he saw in the real world, he was surprised to hear that this picture was recognizable. In fact, the only other *real* thing he tended to sketch was his all-time favorite animal: the finger monkey. About the size of a mouse, finger monkeys are so small that they can wrap around your finger; hence the name. Generally, though, Tim did some of his best work entirely from the depths of his mind. Reality offered just a dash of inspiration. Tim would conjure up distant lands and animals that, to his knowledge, had never existed. His recent creations included a rather compelling bat-dolphin-scissor-pig and a fairly brilliant chalk and charcoal rendition of Bob the Mexican cow-snail. There was a fantastic world, endless and vibrant, enclosed inside the hard cover of his favorite sketch pad.

"Hmm, yes . . . Can you keep a secret?" the man whispered, bringing Tim's attention back. He peered down through thick lenses. "I've come in here to steal a cake. Indeed."

"Me too," Tim said, showing the man his loot, pleased to have a partner in crime.

"I didn't see you, and you didn't see me, right? Promise?"

"Promise." Before he turned to leave, Tim wondered what a person like this—clearly some kind of professor— was doing here. "So, why are you at the Dawn Star?" he asked.

"Ah, now"—the man shook his head—"let's just say that, like our little theft, it's top-secret. . . ."

CHAPTER 2

Tim's bedroom, formally room twenty, had exactly the same layout as all the other guest suites in the building but looked more "lived-in," with considerably more mess. Sitting cross-legged on the end of his bed, he put the final touches on his drawing, turning Elisa's accidental watermark into a puddle on the pavement.

The phone on his bedside table rang. It was Elisa, calling him for dinner. She often contacted him on the hotel's internal system. This made Tim feel even more like a guest and less like her son. Elisa and Chris Green, who ran the Dawn Star, had adopted him a week or two before they'd moved in. At the time it was a dream come true for them, as Elisa had wanted to run a hotel since she was little. This confused Tim because she never seemed to be happy here—in fact, just the opposite. She was constantly anxious, spending much of her time upset about money, about how hard things were, or about how she didn't have time for any of Tim's nonsense—"nonsense" being virtually anything Tim said or did. This worked out quite nicely, as he'd much rather have sat by himself in some corner somewhere than be forced to spend time with Elisa.

As for Chris, well, Tim liked him a lot, but they were very rarely together, as Chris spent most of his time away on business. Working for some Internet company, he was regularly jetting around the world, to sell or buy or look at or talk about . . . stuff. But when he was at the hotel, he was always asking what Tim was up to, and he *always* cared about the answer. It was funny to think that Chris would be the ideal parent if he were there more, and Elisa would be the ideal parent if she were there less.

And although Tim knew the adoption was a permanent arrangement, that they had indeed signed documents meaning they were his legal guardians in every sense, he still couldn't help feeling as though they might not be his parents forever. Sooner or later, he suspected, he'd be thrown back into one of the countless institutions through which he'd passed.

More than anything, though, Tim found the hotel a rather dull place, despite the corridor of lava. Even a brother or sister might have brightened things up.

"I'm too busy for children," Elisa had said, sighing, when he'd suggested that. She'd followed it with a guilty frown, as, of course, Tim knew this to be all too true.

Chris and Elisa occupied what used to be the biggest room in the hotel, which had been converted into living quarters when the Greens had taken over. There they'd meet as a "family" to enjoy a quiet and generally tense meal together.

That night was no different. Elisa moaned for a while about the fact that the hotel's head chef was leaving, and complained about how expensive things were getting, particularly the new security cameras that she was having installed, and the added costs of the consultant she'd hired. She also told Tim that an important guest was staying in room nineteen, opposite his bedroom, so he should be quiet.

Chris had cooked, which meant the food was questionable. The sausages looked like coal, and the mash was . . . well, Tim couldn't be sure if it even was potato. He much preferred it when Elisa cooked, even if it created extra tension.

After dinner Tim returned to his bedroom, and the moment he closed the door, he heard some commotion in the hallway. Using his swivel chair, which he knelt on after rolling it across his carpet, he looked through the peephole. He spotted a man outside room nineteen carrying a huge cardboard box. It was the scientist, his cake-thief friend, and clearly the person Elisa had mentioned. Tim was intrigued. The old man was fumbling with the lock while balancing the giant box in his other hand. It looked far too heavy for him, and he seemed all the more comical through the peephole—distorted and stretched.

"Come on, you slippery, wiggly little . . . ," the old man mumbled. The key tumbled from his hand.

Tim clambered off his chair and opened his door.

"Would you like some help with that?" he asked.

The man turned slowly, straining his neck. He smiled as best he could, the weight of the box visible on his face.

"Ah, hello. Indeed, yes, if you could retrieve the key, there, on the floor." He pointed with a tilt of his head and a madman's wink. Tim crouched and picked it up.

"Now, yes," he continued, "if you could throw it into my mouth, I think I might be able to unlock the door with my teeth. . . ." Leaning forward, he held his lips open and waited.

"Um, I could . . . just open the door for you?"

"Hmm, no . . . wait . . . Yes! Much better idea. Let's do that."

After Tim had let him in, the man carefully placed the

cardboard box on the floor and stood up straight with a groan. "Oh, oh, that's better. . . . Nice to get my back upright again. It's you, isn't it? It is." He squinted through his glasses.

"It's me?"

"You, yes, indeed, the boy. I hope you kept your promise and didn't tell anyone about . . ."

"I didn't. Although, Elisa saw chocolate on my face, so *I* was discovered." All hell had broken loose over dinner. Elisa had said Tim never did as he was told and never listened to what she said . . . or something like that.

"Oh yes, of course . . . wait . . . Elisa?" He frowned.

"She's the owner, the manager," Tim said.

"The manager of the brownies? What a fine job."

"No." Tim laughed. "She's the manager of the hotel. My adoptive mother. She takes care of me. Well, she feeds me and provides me with a room to sleep in."

"Oh yes, yes. I know Elisa. I am glad you kept your promise. A promise between friends . . . oh my, it is not to be broken. I am George Eisenstone," he said, extending his hand to Tim.

"Timothy Hart."

They shook hands.

"Elisa said I shouldn't disturb you," Tim added, turning to leave.

"Ah, no, no." He smiled. "This is my room. I have paid

13

no small sum to stay here. Indeed. It is up to me who comes and goes. Besides, you, well, helped me with my box."

"She told me not to annoy you."

"No doubt she told you not to steal a cake too. You are not annoying me, young man. No, no." Eisenstone sat on the bed, removed his glasses, and began cleaning them with a small yellow square of soft-looking material.

The only thing as deep as Tim's imagination was his curiosity. "So, what's in the box?" he asked.

Eisenstone glanced over his shoulder. "In there is my work. It is very important."

The vague answers were simply making him more excited. "And what, exactly, is that?"

"Secrets." The professor smiled. "At any rate, I fear it won't be terribly interesting. My work isn't . . . it isn't finished. Now . . ." Eisenstone pulled a small silver watch from his top pocket to check the time. "I must go. I have arrangements."

"Okay."

"It was nice to meet you," the professor said, standing.

On the way out Tim peered over for one last quick glance. He struggled with his inquisitive nature at the best of times, but a big mysterious box filled solely with secrets? This was some kind of torture.

The moment he returned to his room, he knelt back on top of his swivel chair and watched the professor leave.

This man *was* intriguing, Tim concluded, still staring through the peephole. Out of the ordinary, and certainly worth investigating—

Hang on.

A strip of natural light escaped into the hall from room nineteen. The door was open, only a sliver, but open nonetheless. Professor Eisenstone must have assumed the first click meant it was locked. In actual fact these old doors needed quite a tug before they would close completely.

Interesting. . . .

Again, Tim left his bedroom and stood for a moment alone in the corridor, biting his thumbnail as he evaluated the temptation.

Could he?

He couldn't. It wouldn't be right.

But . . . maybe . . . maybe just a quick peek. What was the worst that could happen?

He pushed the door open a tiny amount and sneaked a look inside the room. The cardboard box was on the bed, on its side. It was empty. He stopped for a moment and considered turning back. If Professor Eisenstone returned, he'd be angry—he might even tell Elisa. But maybe just a little farther, Tim thought.

On the floor, he saw some wires. Red, white, green, blue, and striped ones all tangled and bunched together with elastic bands. His gaze followed the cables to a large silver contraption sitting on top of the wooden chest of drawers next to the bed. It looked like a microwave, only . . . different. There were exposed circuit boards and a forest of complicated-looking buttons and settings on top. Whatever it was, it looked homemade and unfinished. A small hatch on the top of the box caught Tim's eye. He slid a metal lock, like one from a bathroom, and lifted the lid. The machine was hollow, empty. What does this thing do? Tim silently wondered.

Below him, resting on the carpet, was what looked like a very unusual hat plugged into the box. Before Tim could stop himself, the helmet had found its way onto his head.

It felt heavy and uncomfortable as he continued inspecting the main part of the machine. On the top right-hand side was one button that stood out. It had nothing written on it, but it was big, circular, and green—green being the universal color for "Go," and circles, well, they're just an all-around nice shape.

Then, with no conscious thought, Tim's hand moved forward and pressed the button.

Whoops.

There was a quiet beep when he pulled his arm away. He waited a second, watching a small blue light flash on the top of the device, but nothing happened.

Tim sighed, disappointed to have come this far and still be no closer to knowing what this thing was. The clock on the wall gently ticked. With his tongue Tim picked at his teeth, briefly recalling Chris's recent attempt at dinner. Swallowing, he winced at the taste, thinking of those terrible, crunchy, burned-black sausages. They were just—

With another, louder beep the box lit up and started vibrating on the chest of drawers. Tim stepped back, alarmed. The box groaned, shook, and clacked an orchestra of sounds. Quickly he yanked the hat thing off his head and dropped it onto the floor, taking another step away. Buzzing and shuffling and clattering around on top of the wood, the box seemed alive. For a good twenty seconds it noisily did *something*.

Eventually the machine stuttered and hummed slowly to silence, like a vacuum cleaner whirring down. All the other lights faded, but the tiny blue bulb continued to flash.

After pausing to make sure the odd cube had definitely finished whatever it was it had been doing, he approached. It sat there peacefully, a tiny lick of steam escaping from a vent at the back. There was a vague smell, like his computer's fan. A dusty, plastic, electric odor.

Tim put his hand on the little hatch on top, felt that it was warm, and began to open—

"TIMOTHY HART!" someone screamed.

He swung round, like a deer in headlights, to see Elisa in the doorway.

• • •

Back in his bedroom, the shouting had been rumbling in the background for some time.

"No drawing for a week," Elisa announced. This caught his attention. "There's nothing else I can do to punish you, Tim. I can't ground you—you've not got any friends." Her eyes darted to the ground as she turned away. Tim suspected that she regretted saying that, but it didn't slow her down as she collected his drawing stuff. She even yanked all the paper out of the printer. Finally she'd lost it.

"Elisa, I wouldn't dream of criticizing your disciplinary techniques," he began cautiously. "I *completely* understand why you're doing this, I do get it. But you're supposed to encourage children's creativity. Stopping me from drawing is probably not a good idea."

He wasn't as bothered as he should have been about this. He had backup pencils and paper stashed all over the place.

"Of course *you* don't think it's a good idea; that's the point of a punishment."

She finished gathering up his things, tossed them into a trash bag, and then opened the door. Across the hall Tim saw the professor arriving at his room.

"Ah," Elisa said. "Mr. Eisenstone, just the man I want to speak to. Tim, come here and say sorry this instant."

After a couple of false starts, Tim tentatively explained.

"Hmm." Eisenstone thought for a moment. "Apology accepted."

"Upstairs, now," Elisa said. "You can do *all* the washing-up today."

Truthfully, Tim *was* sorry. Not because he had broken the rules but because he had betrayed the professor's trust. Soon, however, none of this would matter, as, unbeknownst to Tim, something that would change the world forever was waiting for Eisenstone in room nineteen.

CHAPTER 3

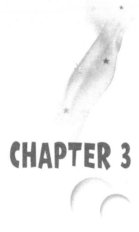

As part of his punishment for trespassing in Eisenstone's room, Tim was forced to wash and dry a frankly absurd number of plates, pots, and pans in Chris and Elisa's living quarters. When he was finished, he returned straight to his bedroom, where a small piece of paper had been slipped under his door.

He picked it up and unfolded it to read, "Tim, come and see me when you get this note. George Eisenstone."

It was signed with the most magnificent signature Tim had ever seen. It covered much of the small, lined sheet. The G in "George" spiraled wildly and whipped across to the top of the E in "Eisenstone."

Wondering why he'd been summoned, Tim knocked on room nineteen's thick wooden door.

The professor let him in. "Sit down, Tim," he said, perching on the corner of his bed and gesturing at a chair in the corner.

It was hard to judge his mood. He didn't *seem* particularly angry, but as Tim took a seat, he felt the need to apologize all over again.

"I'm really, really sorry," he said. "I just saw that your door was—"

"Tim, Tim, it's fine, I don't mind. In your shoes I would have done the same. Indeed. Curiosity is . . . well . . . a good thing; don't listen when people tell you it isn't."

"Okay." Tim was a little confused.

"But, buttery but, but, but, let me ask you something, and it's important that you're honest. . . . *What* were you thinking when you pressed the button?" He pointed at the device in the corner. Tim had been making a special effort not to look at it.

"I am really sorry. I don't know what came over me." Tim's voice was jittery—he didn't like being told off. (Apart from by Elisa. He sort of enjoyed that in a weird way.)

"No, no. Tim. No. You misunderstand. I am asking you why you did what you did. Tell me, literally, indeed, *what* you were thinking the moment you pressed that button. . . . You were wearing the reader, yes?"

"The reader?" Tim asked.

"The reader. The hat thingy. The . . . thing . . . you put on your head."

"I . . ." Tim looked at the floor, ashamed.

"Yes." Eisenstone leaned forward, eager for the information.

"I . . . I was thinking . . . I don't know." Tim searched his brain. He closed his eyes to remember. "I thought about how silly I looked. I saw myself in the mirror. The hat, helmet, reader thing, it was too big for me. I was scared Elisa would come in. I was scared *you* would come in. But I pressed the button and then waited and there was a long pause. . . . I thought about . . . about . . . I looked at the clock. . . . Then I, I picked some food out of my teeth."

"Yes!" Eisenstone yelled, overly excited, leaning even closer. "And what did you think?"

"It was, um, I thought about dinner. I thought about how bad a cook Chris is."

"YES! Why? What's wrong with his cooking?"

Tim opened his eyes. "Everything. I mean, don't get me wrong, Chris is a great guy, but his food is bordering on illegal. If social services came by, I'd hide it. He has this habit of making the most disgusting, horrid, hard, dry, black, burned-to-a-crisp—"

"Let me guess," Eisenstone whispered, lifting his brow. "Sausages?"

"Yes," Tim replied in surprise.

The professor's face lit up as he stood, clapping his hands. He grabbed Tim by the shoulders.

"This is amazing!" he yelled, shaking him. "Indeed. Do you know what this means?"

"I really don't."

Excitement had possessed Eisenstone. He began to pace, mumbling to himself. Pointing to the ceiling, he stopped and turned to Tim.

"You have no idea how incredible you are, do you?"

"I've had my suspicions." Tim wasn't sure what the professor was rambling on about, but he smiled nonetheless.

"What you've done is . . ." Eisenstone looked around the room for the right words. "Brilliant!" He clenched his fists. "You're a genius, my boy. A genius. Although, it must be secret. For now. But then when it's written up and complete. Patents and studies all done. My word. When it's all complete. The potential. The implications!"

"Professor Eisenstone," Tim said calmly, "what is so exciting?"

"I'll *show* you!"

The contraption was open, and on the side next to it was a shoe box, from which Eisenstone removed something, before flicking the cardboard lid across the room. He hurried back and stood in front of Tim, clutching a sandwich bag.

"Hold out your hand," he said.

Tim did as he was told, still seated and still frankly

nervous about all this unexplained joy. A shriveled-up sausage, wrapped in plastic, dropped into Tim's palm.

The professor nodded manically, biting his fist in anticipation. "It's a sausage!" he sang.

"Yes," Tim said, frowning. "A burned one."

Everything had all gotten a bit odd, and Tim was starting to think Eisenstone might actually be crazy, just a mentally ill old man. Sad, really. Maybe he'd recently escaped from somewhere. Maybe he was the professor of Crayon Digestion at the University of Loopyville.

"I've run tests," Eisenstone continued. "It's made of pork, a few herbs, and spices. Traces of salt, of water— believe it or not, all the ingredients you'd need to make a sausage." The professor grabbed Tim again and knelt, staring intensely. "All the ingredients."

"Forgive me, again, but what on earth is so amazing about a sausage?"

"Nothing. Absolutely nothing. But a sausage you've made appear, using only your mind and my device. Indeed, *that,* my boy, is amazing."

"I see." Tim glanced to the door. "Wait, hang on. That sausage was in your machine . . . thing? But I checked inside before I did anything. It was empty."

"Yes, it *was.* That's the whole point."

"What *is* that box?" Tim whispered.

Arms out, flapping like wings, Eisenstone danced over to the contraption, where he then stood proudly.

"This, young Timothy, is an atomic arrangement vessel." He held his hands out and widened his eyes, as though Tim were supposed to understand.

"A whaty what what?"

"And, because of you, it actually works."

"What does an atom . . . arrangement . . . thing actually do?"

"Ah!" Eisenstone turned to the device. "A fine question indeed. Well, essentially, what happens is, millions of airborne nanomachines equipped with primitive artificial intelligence construct any item one can imagine . . . with certain restraints. Oh yes. Quite."

"Right," Tim said, raising an eyebrow.

"You see, I am a theoretical particle physicist. Yes. Yes. Energy, motion, space, and time." He clicked his fingers. "And *this* is my invention. I call it the Thought-Directed Atomic Construction Device. Or a TDACD for short."

"So, it . . . it reads your thoughts and then makes . . . *constructs* whatever you imagine?"

"Precisely."

"Hang on," Tim added. "If I imagined, say, a pencil with this hat . . . helmet—"

"Reader."

"With this reader thing on my head, and pressed the button, you're telling me a pencil would appear inside?"

"Tim," Eisenstone said, nodding, "that's *exactly* what I'm telling you."

"Wow."

"Although, honestly, no one has yet been able to successfully make an object. Even tiny ones, a few atoms big, have been a struggle. It's the signals . . . from the brain . . . electromagnetic . . . I mean . . ." He seemed to wince at how complicated it was. "To have the clarity of thought you have . . . and something so complex. A sausage! Cooked to imperfection. It's all been theory up until you came along."

"Hmm." Tim nodded, wandering over. "May I?" he asked with his hand above the box, keen to inspect it again, now that he knew its potential.

"Go ahead."

Lifting the lid, Tim saw that little electronic components lined the inside. Excitement bubbled as his mind came alive with all the possible things he could conjure.

"And what did you say you call it?" he asked.

"A Thought-Directed Atomic Construction Device. Indeed." Eisenstone tilted his head and exhaled. "TDACD."

"You should have a shorter name for it," Tim said, holding the reader in his hands.

"Hmm. I've done brainstorms, you know, whiteboards, spidergrams, the works. The name is . . . it's a winner."

"Nah. Call it . . . ," Tim said, thinking. "Call it the Imagination Box."

CHAPTER 4

Tim, of course, had wanted to start imagining things straightaway, but the professor had insisted on waiting until they were both in his lab—a "secure, private, and scientific" environment.

The following day, after a short drive across Glassbridge, Eisenstone and Tim arrived at what looked like an old industrial estate. However, one brand-new building, clad in modern pine and lightly tinted glass, stood out from all the rest. This was the professor's place of work, and Tim was keen to get inside and try the Imagination Box again—properly this time.

That morning the professor had had a quick chat with

Elisa, and had told her he needed Tim to help with a study at his laboratory. Worrying that she might see this as an opportunity for further punishment for his trespassing in room nineteen, Tim tried not to show his excitement at the prospect. Luckily, she didn't seem to mind. Her thoughts had clearly been elsewhere. She'd been tied up chatting with Donald Pinkman, the hotel's new consultant, whom she'd hired to make things run more smoothly.

Inside the large building, Eisenstone seemed to relax. They passed through countless corridors and five checkpoints, all of which required him to show ID and to swipe a card. It gave Tim the sense that a lot of important and groundbreaking work must have gone on in this sprawling complex.

During the car ride there, Tim had stared out the window and wondered aloud why, if it was so important that the box remained a secret, the professor was keeping it in the hotel.

"There must be more suitable places," Tim had said. "I mean, I got my hands on it."

"As fate would have it, indeed."

Besides Tim's trespass, the Dawn Star Hotel was, the professor had explained, "perhaps the most secure place of all."

"Burglar alarms, modern security cameras, both private *and* public," he had said. "It is maybe the safest place for me, and for the invention. But, indeed, perhaps I've become too comfortable, complacent, letting down my guard. At any rate, as lovely as the establishment is, I assure you, Tim, this is no holiday for me."

After what seemed a mile of walking down long corridors, they arrived at a final door, which hissed open following a card swipe. Gradually one bulb after another flickered on until the room was illuminated by clean white light.

Tim had seen spaces like this in countless sci-fi films, but this one was better, neater, and minimalist.

"Ah, yes, you can tell I've not been here for a while," Eisenstone said. "Look how tidy it is."

While he unpacked and prepared, Tim tried to wait patiently near the door, but the temptation to go off exploring grew unbearable. About eleven seconds later, he ventured deeper into the lab.

There was the usual kind of equipment, test tubes and beakers, and also a number of gadgets and electronic bits and pieces, all housed on pedestals and in transparent boxes, like exhibits in a museum. As Tim threaded his way through the room, running his fingers along the desks—making two legs out of his index and middle—he guessed that most of the items he saw were in some way related to the Imagination Box. The whole place seemed dedicated to it. Years and years of groundbreaking work was on display.

He arrived at a workstation with a wide computer screen, surrounded by notes and photos. Sunlight drew horizontal lines across the wood, striped by the slats in the window's blind. Specs of dust danced, only visible in the glowing layers of air.

"Who is this?" Tim asked, holding up a framed picture of a girl around his age.

"Ah, quite. That is Dee, my granddaughter," Eisenstone said, walking over to him. "She's about your age—eleven come March. She's in my garden, see." He tapped on the picture frame's glass.

Dee was wearing a red polka-dot dress and standing among a number of exotic-looking flowers, in front of an autumn sunset. She had Professor Eisenstone's ever-so-slightly manic smile.

"You have a nice garden."

"Yes, quite."

"Is it far away?"

"My garden?" Eisenstone said. "No, it's near Winter Church. But as I said before, my home isn't a great place to be at the moment, certainly not in light of recent break-throughs. Too dangerous."

"Dangerous?" Tim frowned.

"Oh yes. There are forces afoot that would move heaven and earth for this prototype, indeed." He placed the frame back on the desk, proudly straightening it. "And, yes, Dee's a good girl, very clever. She's an all-right artist, like you. Creative does seem to be the default setting for children."

"So, do you think she could use the box?" Tim asked. "Has she tried?"

"I . . . I wouldn't feel comfortable testing it on her," Eisenstone said.

"Why?"

"It's . . . complicated. I wouldn't have let you try it either, had you not done so by yourself."

The Imagination Box was set on a table; next to it was a laptop with a microphone plugged in, a digital camcorder, and two stools, awaiting Tim and Eisenstone. They both sat.

"Okay, now, yes, right, let's—" A phone on the wall began to ring. "Quite perfect timing," the professor sighed. "Hello," he said into the handset as he tugged at the curly cord.

Tim couldn't hear who was on the other end or what they said, but Eisenstone's face went a peculiar shade of gray as his smile disappeared.

"Okay," he said. "Bring him down."

He returned to the table and perched on the stool.

"Tim, we'll have to carry on in a little bit. I have an important guest. A policeman."

A few minutes later, the door buzzed, hissed, and

clunked open, and a security guard Tim had seen earlier entered. He was followed by a chubby man wearing a long, light brown coat with a shirt and tie underneath.

Eisenstone thanked the guard, who departed, leaving the guest behind.

"George," the large man said, shaking hands.

"Inspector Kane," the professor replied.

They walked into the corner and spoke in hushed voices. Tim couldn't hear what was being said. The policeman had short brown hair, stubble, and tired-looking eyes. At one point he got something from his pocket, and Tim spotted the corner of a bronze-colored badge, mounted on leather, holstered on his belt.

As they spoke, Inspector Kane looked over, made eye contact, and smiled warmly. Tim snapped his gaze to the laptop in front of him in an effort to pretend he wasn't staring.

Eisenstone and the inspector's chat ended, and the security guard returned and escorted the policeman out of the room.

"Yes, yes, sorry about that," Eisenstone said, returning to his seat.

"Was it bad news?" Tim asked, unable to resist being nosy.

"No. Well, yes and no. As I said, Inspector Kane is a policeman. You see, my briefcase was stolen from me a few weeks ago, and he's following up on some leads. All my notes, my work, all gone. Goney gone gone. It was taken from my home, and I, for one, don't believe it was opportunistic."

"What do you mean?"

"I . . ." Eisenstone seemed suddenly saddened. He sighed and cringed at a memory. "It's complex, but I . . . You see, I had an old friend, Professor Whitelock. We shared much of our career together. We were . . . academic partners. Yes. For years we'd been working on this very thing, on an atomic constructor, an Imagination Box. We were making real progress. But a couple of months ago he . . . sadly, he died."

"Oh." Tim was surprised to hear that the invention had a rocky history. He had expected such a device to have come about in a fairy-tale kind of way—spark of inspiration, bit of computer stuff, soldering, some packing tape, done.

"Yes. Well, Whitelock went a bit . . . shall we say . . . odd. They say there's a fine line between genius and madness. Well, Professor Whitelock was certainly a genius, but it seemed he also crossed the line. He became ill. He . . . he lost his mind."

"Lost his mind? Ketchup on cornflakes or . . . ?"

"Worse. You see, we drifted apart, and I hadn't heard from him for a fair while . . . and then there was an incident. A fire at his laboratory. He was killed, maybe murdered, and much of his . . . much of *our* work was lost.

33

True enough, we'd not been close toward the end, but I still miss him every day. Tragically, he'd just gotten married too. Very sad times indeed. The point is, although it has never been proven, I don't think his death was an accident."

"Someone started the fire deliberately?"

"I suspect so."

"Why?" Tim had heard of academic rivals, but arson? Murder? This seemed altogether more serious.

"I feel it was to cover up a theft. For many years he'd been working on a teleporter."

"Really?" What other incredible gadgets was the professor involved with? Tim wondered.

"Yes, the technology, you understand, is not dissimilar from the Imagination Box. To teleport something you must first break it down, in essence destroy it, and then re-create it at another location. Rumor had it that he'd successfully teleported a live owl."

"Wow."

"Indeed. And, well, very few people knew what he was up to, so when the police discovered his lab burned down—his work destroyed—they wouldn't have been looking for a missing teleporter. In fact, they ignored it entirely. I tried to tell them that it had been stolen, but my words fell on deaf ears. I'm not sure the police ever really believed me."

"So someone killed him just to steal his teleporter?"

Eisenstone exhaled with a shrug. "I just can't be sure. I might be paranoid—it might be silly of me to seek refuge in the Dawn Star. But I've been burgled twice now, and both times my notes have been taken. I just have this terrible feeling that whoever targeted Whitelock might be targeting me."

Now Tim could see real worry in the professor's eyes, and he had a sudden pang of fear himself, wondering if he too was in any kind of danger. However, as he watched Eisenstone prepare the Imagination Box for testing, there was no denying that this was also alluring.

"Anyway, enough about all that. We've got work to do, yes?" The professor pulled a large notepad from his satchel and began patting himself down.

"Now, Tim, you don't happen to have a pencil on you?"

"Always," Tim replied, pulling a tiny red pencil from his shirt pocket. "I don't go anywhere without one."

"Oh yes, I'm the same with this," Eisenstone replied, sliding his silver watch out of his pocket and placing it on the desk between them.

"That's nice." Tim picked it up and flipped it over. Engraved on the back were the letters *PE*. He ran his finger across the initials, feeling the depth of the carving.

"Peter Eisenstone was my father. Yes. He gave me this when I was about your age. Or a bit younger. Or older.

Indeed. That watch has never left my side. I don't go anywhere without it."

"I need a watch," Tim said, sliding it back across the wood.

"Maybe *your* father will—" Eisenstone realized what he was saying and stopped himself. "Sorry."

"It's fine. Maybe I'll make one in the machine," Tim said, and laughed.

The professor paused, fiddling with the corner of his notepad. His eyes drifted away and then swept back to Tim.

"What happened to your parents?" he said cautiously. "If you don't mind my asking?"

Surprised by the question—people rarely asked—Tim shuffled in his seat. "Um . . . well . . . my mother died when I was a baby, and then my father disappeared. I lived with some people and then some others and then some others and now Chris and Elisa. Strange, isn't it?"

"Oh yes, my, yes, very."

"Sometimes people just disappear and never return. Really, it happens a lot. Look it up. Hundreds of people go missing every year and don't come back. I sometimes wonder where my father is, and then I realize that if he's still alive, he doesn't want to be found, and if he's dead, he can't be. So there's no point in my worrying about it."

Eisenstone slowly nodded. He seemed to respect Tim's

attitude. "You really do remind me of Dee," he said, moving his notepad to one side. "Righto. Now we go to the fun bit. The bit with all the fun. Let's start with a marble, Tim. Indeed, can you do that?"

The professor placed the reader on Tim's head, adjusted some wiring, and then pressed the button.

"Just as before," he said. "Just imagine it."

Scrunching his face, Tim closed his eyes, focusing hard on keeping his mind clear of other thoughts, ignoring all sounds, just thinking about marbles.

But nothing happened.

He looked around, bewildered. Eisenstone pouted, frowning a little. Again, Tim closed his eyes and tried—really concentrating now. His mind took a few moments to completely craft the image a second time, and then, finally, like a key turning in a lock, the infinite variations he *could* have imagined slipped away, and a picture of a perfect glass sphere settled. A swirl of blue spiraled through the core, and a spectacular gloss rolled across the surface.

The machine rumbled to life, buzzing and clunking, hissing and vibrating as it did its constructing. Tim and the professor watched the small blue light on top of the Imagination Box return to flashing, signaling completion. Then the professor slid the lock open and pulled the lid back, while Tim tensely chewed his thumb.

What if there were nothing in there at all? What if he couldn't do it a second time? He found himself holding his breath as Eisenstone stared silently into the box.

Please let it work.

Slowly the professor slipped back onto his stool, a single tear falling from his cheek.

"Are you okay?" Tim asked, concerned. *It hadn't worked.*

"Tim . . . ," Eisenstone said, "this is the happiest moment of my life. This *is* very good indeed." He stood and turned away, clearly overwhelmed by the moment. The old man's shoulders lifted a little, up and down. At first Tim thought he was crying, but then he heard rising laughter.

With a knee on the desk, Tim leaned over to look. Sure enough, a marble lay at the bottom of the box, resting in the corner of the metal interior. He'd done it.

Around five, Eisenstone drove them back to the hotel. They pulled in to the parking lot behind the building, next to the alleyway leading to the back of the kitchen. From here Tim could see his bedroom window. Steam rose from a vent, and a slight smell of dinner filled the lot.

"Can I ask you one more favor, Tim?" Eisenstone said in a serious tone.

"Yes."

"Please, please don't tell anyone specifically what we've been doing. Not even Chris or Elisa. It's important. Very, very."

"Um . . . okay." Tim had no trouble with white lies when it came to Elisa—they were his bread and butter. Lying to Chris was never as easy, but he'd respect Eisenstone's wishes, despite the temptation.

"Soon, soon, soon, when it's all put together and we know it works—"

"It does work."

"It's . . . it's early days still. This is a big deal, Tim. This will change . . . everything. Once we understand the technology a bit better, we can ensure it is safe. In the right hands, this could be a revolutionary machine. In the wrong hands, well, it could be catastrophic."

CHAPTER 5

"So I can make, say, a spoon?"

"Yes."

"Could I make . . . a cow?"

"No. Yes. Well . . . potentially, yes, a small one. Or in a bigger machine, it's possible you could make a cow. It's complex, but yes, essentially, yes. Not in this prototype, of course."

It was day two of their experimenting at the lab. Eisenstone had just made them both a hot chocolate—the regular way—and was attempting to explain the physical nature of the universe. He said he wanted Tim to understand the science behind the Imagination Box before they made the next item. There were also plans to test Tim's brain, to take various readings.

"Matter. It's a tricky concept to get your head around," Eisenstone said. "You see, me, you, everyone, everything, we're made of stuff. Made of bits of stuff. That stuff was made in the stars a long time ago, and it has just been arranged in lots of different ways. Like a supermarket that has eggs, flour, and sugar inside. Everything you need to make a cake. Humans, well, we're made mostly of water, which is made of oxygen and hydrogen. Then there is some carbon, calcium, nitrogen, and a few other bits and pieces. The point is, it's *stuff.* Everything is. Think of the world like that, and well, indeed, it's remarkably wonderful."

"I see," Tim replied, nodding, looking briefly at his own hand. He glanced at the device, wondering silently what he would make if he were given a free go. There were countless options.

Eisenstone stood and took his hot chocolate over to his other desk. He started tapping away on the computer with his back to Tim, who was still on the bench with the Imagination Box in front of him. Annoyingly, the professor was in no rush to make things and was forcing Tim to be patient while he typed up endless notes. After all, he'd been working on this gadget for years. However, Tim was growing impatient. Half of him wanted to conduct himself like a scientist, going slowly, one step at a time, recording findings as he went. La, la, la. But he also just wanted to get that reader on and see what he could make. And, more important, see what he *couldn't* make.

"How about a potato?" Tim asked with a shrug.

"Yes, even easier than a cow."

"A jar of . . . jam?"

"Yes."

"A jar of . . . salad dressing?"

"Yes."

"A jar of . . . anger."

"Yes. Wait . . . no. No."

"Not a jar of anger?"

"Nothing abstract. I think, no. Anything concrete. A rock, yes. A shoelace, yes. Happiness, no. Ambition, no, I don't presume so. These are not solid, tangible things. I would deduce from my research, indeed, that you could make a custard-flavored belt, for instance, or a sock filled with rainbow-colored tea leaves, but try to make a bubble of maybe, or an eggcup filled with lies, and you'll run into trouble. Indeed, anything you could pick up . . ."

"*Any*thing?"

"Well. No. Weightless lead or hot ice, these are not possible. It mustn't conflict with the laws of physics. It can't be . . . it can't be *impossible*."

Tim was fiddling idly with the helmet, entangling his

42

fingers in the wires. "I guess that depends on the definition of the word."

"Oh yes, lovely, yes, I admire your thinking," Eisenstone said, turning his body on his stool. "There is something quite excellent about the way your mind works. I guess it's only with age that we gain restrictions. Yes, quite poetic, isn't it?"

"What if the limits were just our imagination?" Tim had something in mind.

"Now, now, I hate to disappoint you, Tim, but the Imagination Box isn't magic—it does have restrictions. Remember, what it does is simply build things, like if you made a house from LEGOs. Except it uses atoms instead."

Tim looked over to Eisenstone, who was still facing away, absorbed in his computer. "I could make anything out of LEGOs, if I had enough bricks," Tim said, placing the reader on his head.

Lifting a finger, he thought of the one thing he'd always wanted, one thing he'd dreamed of during those long afternoons, one thing he'd sketched time and time again. Wearing the metal helmet, he visualized his next creation, reached out, and pressed the button.

The beep, the clunk, the whizzing, and the machine was once again alive. Eisenstone shut his laptop and turned to look.

"Oh, Tim, you just couldn't wait, could you?" he said over the noise.

The box settled down, with a puff of steam and the now familiar blue light, Tim's creation inside.

"What have you made?" Eisenstone asked with a half smile.

Without another word, Tim leaned over, clunked the lock open, and gasped as he lifted the lid.

A tiny monkey, no larger than a mouse, leapt out onto the edge of the box.

"It worked!" Tim yelled with joy.

The creature looked up at them, glancing from one to the other frantically as it took in its surroundings. It had brown fur with a striped tail and huge, cautious eyes. It hopped fluidly, like a squirrel, along the top of the machine to one corner, where it peered down, before shuffling back to its original spot. They both watched the incredible animal in absolute amazement.

"I'll call him . . . Phillip, or Phil. Phil the finger monkey," Tim said, leaning in for a closer look. "Seems a reasonable name."

Cautiously the creature reached up and touched Tim's nose with one of its absurdly small hands. With a giggle, Tim flinched, and the monkey scurried away a little on the lid. Then, tentatively, it returned to the edge, inspecting Tim's face.

After a moment of quiet contemplation of its creator, the

finger monkey relaxed, glanced around at the space near the box, and then leapt onto the desk. It went straight for Tim's hot chocolate, fishing out a marshmallow and experimentally nibbling on the corner. Eisenstone and Tim remained transfixed as the animal sat merrily devouring the squishy sweet.

"It is . . . utterly *incredible,* Tim." Eisenstone was clearly baffled. "An organism. So complicated, so perfect. It's intelligent, it's . . . I . . . *Indeed* . . . I never even considered that *this* machine could be used to make living creatures. To create *life.*"

The tiny animal stopped to look directly into the professor's eyes, which stared back adoringly, large behind their lenses.

"Hello, little monkey," Eisenstone said, leaning closer.

"Hello?" Phil replied clearly.

Tim's eyes and mouth widened in unison. It had worked.

Arms flopping by his side, the professor stood, knocking his stool back onto the floor. "Pardon?" he said, turning his head as if he was scared of the answer.

"I said . . . ah, hello," Phil replied in an elegantly posh voice, just as Tim had imagined.

Eisenstone pulled his glasses from his face, dropped them onto the desk, and then rubbed his forehead, placing his other palm on the table next to Phil. Tim looked between them, frankly enjoying the professor's reaction.

"You . . . you can . . . No. You can't . . . but you can."

Eisenstone was flabbergasted. "You can talk. Indeed you seem to be able to talk. But you surely . . . No."

"It certainly seems so," Phil replied with a smile. He scurried back to the marshmallow. "Now, not another word from me until you chaps explain what this extravagantly beautiful thing is."

The monkey dragged the sweet along the desk; it was half his size, so it seemed to be a little bit of a struggle.

"It's a marshmallow," Tim said. He remembered the daydreams he'd had, time and time again, when he'd imagined what it might be like to have the best pet on earth, but he hadn't dared to think it would be *this* good.

"Well, it is delicious, and I thank you for it."

"Care to try the hot chocolate?" Tim asked, quickly accepting that Phil could talk. He was surprised, sure, but deep down he had expected it to work. If Tim had faith in *anyone,* it was himself.

"May I?" Phil asked, turning his tiny head back to the cup.

After dipping his little finger into the hot chocolate, Tim dangled a drop above Phil.

"That is most amazing. Can you acquire more?" he asked, licking his lips.

"Yep, as much as you want. There's even nicer hot chocolate at the hotel where I live. This stuff isn't actually that good." He turned to Eisenstone. "No offense."

46

"It gets better? Impossible." Phil's minuscule claws tapped on the surface of the desk as he scurried to the mug, where he clambered up the side and plunged his furry face into its contents, slurping and groaning with pleasure. "It is so tasty. Hot and chocolatey in equally delightful measure. This is surely the greatest thing in this strange world."

Eisenstone hadn't moved for quite a while now. A couple of times his mouth closed for a moment as if he were about to speak, but then he just lifted his brow and went back to the same position, chin dangling.

Leaving a trail of soon-to-be-sticky drips, Phil ran back across the desk. He moved on all fours, slightly sideways, slightly forward, just like a monkey a hundred times his size.

"What else is there?" Phil asked, looking over his shoulder. "What is the meaning of that box? Where am I? Who are you? I am so very confused. But excited too. Confused and excited. It is about fifty-fifty at present. I must confess, it is quite a pleasant sensation."

"Stop," Eisenstone said finally. "You can't talk."

Sharing a look with Tim, who gave a quick shrug, Phil laughed.

"Now, sir, I am just as confused as you are—perhaps more so. But I do appear to be able to talk, quite articulately, if I do say so myself."

"No, you . . . can't be real. I'm imagining this." Eisenstone shook his head. "Monkeys don't talk. Indeed. And you're a monkey."

"Finger monkey," Tim corrected him.

"But in all seriousness," Phil said, licking the last bits of hot chocolate off his paws, "who is in charge here?" He pointed quickly between Tim and Eisenstone with one tiny little finger. "Am I real or am I not?"

"You are," Tim said, giving him a quick poke. "Definitely."

Eisenstone shook his head.

Phil had a long think. "So, Timothy thinks I am real. I think I am real. I calculate that to be two against one. This is what is called consensus. How do we know anything is real? We just have to come to an agreement."

"This . . . this is . . . astonishing," the professor said.

"It's just a tiny little talking monkey," Tim replied. "Stranger things have happened."

"No, Tim," Eisenstone said. "No, they haven't."

Later, when they'd packed everything up and Phil had found a comfortable home in Tim's red-checkered-shirt pocket, they left the lab. Outside, beyond a chain-link fence, a black car was parked half on the sidewalk, half in the road. As Eisenstone slid the Imagination Box, hidden as always in cardboard, into the trunk of his car, Tim caught a glistening glare out of the corner of his eye—

a reflection off something. The driver, wearing large sunglasses and a green hat, then lowered an object, started his engine, and drove off out of sight. Tim could have sworn the man had been pointing a camera at them.

"Eisenstone, did you see . . . ," Tim said, frowning, steadily wondering if he was just being paranoid.

"Did I see what?" the professor said, dropping the lid of the trunk down with a soft thud. "What is it?" He seemed worried.

"I just . . . Nothing."

Tim climbed in and put his seat belt on. Out of fear or perhaps hope, he decided he hadn't seen it. Maybe, like for a lot of other things that day, his imagination was to blame.

CHAPTER 6

That evening, people milled around in the Dawn Star's lobby, sipping coffee at tables near the window, reading the paper before dinner, and generally doing what hotel guests do—not very much. There was a plan to go back to the lab later that night, and Tim could hardly wait, but first he entered the dining area, walking at a suspiciously slow pace.

Smiling at a waitress, he loitered near the entrance to the kitchen, two swinging doors with little round windows in the tops. The coast looked clear. Tim ducked in and crouched behind the main counter. Just above him dishes were being moved and pots were bubbling. On the other side of the silver surface, five or six chefs were busy at work. Noisily cooking, chatting, pinning orders to the wall, and weaving in and out of each other's space.

Tim crawled on all fours across the tiles, to the back end of the kitchen, the walk-in fridge. He had a quick glance over his cover of cardboard boxes to confirm that no one was watching, then tugged on the large shiny handle, crawled inside the chilled room, and began to search.

Cheesecake, cream, sponge cake . . . Come on. Where was it?

He stopped. There they were: twenty or so little glass bowls filled with a delicious, award-winning dessert. The tiny round sticker on the side of them had the hotel's logo printed on it. The Dawn Star chocolate fudge pudding. Tim grabbed one, wrapped it in some nearby plastic wrap, rammed it into his pocket, and swiftly exited the fridge. Head down, he walked briskly toward the swinging doors.

"Hey!" a voice yelled. "What you doing in my kitchen?"

"I . . ." Tim turned and looked. It was someone he didn't recognize. This must be the new chef Elisa had mentioned, clad in the Dawn Star's whites with a little gold *DS* sewn into the shirt's breast. He was young, perhaps twenty, tall, heavyset, with short black hair and light eyes. "*Your* kitchen?" Tim asked.

The young chef smiled. "You must be Tim," he said. "I'm Stephen Crowfield. Elisa said I might bump into

51

you. She mentioned you've been known to help yourself to certain choice items from the fridge."

Tim put his hand into his pocket, feeling the cool, expensive glass bowl that housed his freshly stolen loot. "Well, frankly, that's slander," he said. "I wouldn't dream of such a thing."

Stephen went along with the lie. "Sure. But maybe I'll make an extra couple of bits and pieces from now on, just in case."

"Hey, Mr. Crowfield, you do what you've got to do to make ends meet."

"Call me Stephen," he said.

"Elisa said I should address members of staff formally."

"Well, I gather you don't always do what she tells you."

"Stephen," Tim said, tilting his head, "you might be right."

The young chef gave him a quick thumbs-up. "See you soon, kid."

Tim turned on his foot and left, thinking that he quite liked Stephen. In comparison he hadn't been fond of the last chef, Antonio, who hadn't taken too kindly to missing produce.

Back he went through the dining room, the treacherous lava hallway, up the stairs to his bedroom, and kicked the door closed behind him.

"Phil?" Tim whispered. "Phil, where are you?"

The monkey was sitting on the laptop's keyboard, looking at various pages on the Internet. His round eyes had massive white squares in them—reflections of the screen in front of him—and his chin dangled in awe.

"Timothy," Phil said, turning his fuzzy little face, "I have been on the so-called World Wide Web learning about this universe of yours, as per your instructions. I have seen some good things and"—he slowly shook his head and looked down—"some bad things. And now I have a few inquiries."

"Okay," Tim replied, sitting on his desk chair in front of the laptop.

Backlit by the computer, Phil swiveled round. Sitting on the keys, not heavy enough to press them without jumping, he fit perfectly, his feet just resting on the space bar, his bum on *G* and *H*.

"Number one," Phil said, frowning in thought, "what is the purpose of a bow tie?"

"I . . . um . . . I'm not sure. . . . It's a strange question. Maybe they used to hold your shirt on, in the olden days? I don't know if they have a purpose as such, just to look smart, I guess."

"This is in line with what I suspected. I think I quite like them. Next, in a cinema, or a theater, which armrest belongs to you? Is it the one on the right, or the one on the left?"

"Again," Tim said, pouting and shrugging, "I don't really know. I don't think there are written rules."

"I see. Perhaps there should be, to avoid disputes." Phil looked down at his feet, wiggling them. "How many toes does a horse have?"

"None. They have hooves."

"Goats?"

"Hooves."

"Bison?"

"Hooves."

"Ducks?"

"Hoo— No, wait. Three? Or one? I don't know . . . I'm not sure."

"Where is Funky Town?"

"Phil, right, I can see this going on for a while. Look, I have a present for you," Tim said.

"Magnificent. Might it be a unicycle, a tiny little unicycle that I could ride around on? Imagine that. The wonder."

Possible, Tim thought, if he had the Imagination Box with him. "Um. No. It's something to eat."

"As in food?" Phil asked.

"Yes, as in food. I remembered how much you liked hot chocolate. So . . ." Tim pulled the pudding from his pocket. "Ta-da. I got you this. It is probably the greatest chocolatey creation of all time."

One of Phil's bulbous eyes narrowed. He was intrigued; he rubbed his chin. "Chocolate, you say?"

Tim pulled the plastic wrap off, and the monkey inspected the pudding. He was just about to dip his paw when there was a loud knock on the door.

"You know the drill," Tim said, pointing at a small paper cup on his desk. Phil scurried over to it and hid himself underneath. This was their well-rehearsed procedure. Tim knew that Phil, like a lot of recent activities, had to be kept a secret.

He opened the door to see Eisenstone.

"Tim, we must talk," he said, waving him toward his own room.

"Phil, it's okay, you can come out."

The cup slid across the desk to the edge, where it tilted and then fell. A small shriek came out as the cup tumbled to the ground. Phil crawled out and brushed himself off, looking slightly embarrassed. After zipping across the carpet, he leapt onto the bed, then onto the bedside table and straight up the spine of the lamp. He then darted with incredible agility along the frame of a painting and finally landed on Tim's shoulder. Tim held his shirt pocket open, and the creature slid into it. Eisenstone smiled, astonished.

They crossed the hall and sat in room nineteen. Phil got out and spent some time climbing up and down the curtain.

The professor slouched with a long sigh before he began to talk.

"Tim, I fear our work might have to be cut short. Things have gotten a little suspicious. I may have been followed this morning. I saw a car."

"Oh." Tim instantly changed his mind about the man he'd seen. It hadn't been just his imagination. "I saw a person, outside the lab. I think he was taking photos of us."

"What?" Eisenstone gasped. "Why didn't you tell me?"

"I didn't see it clearly. I thought . . . I thought maybe I was mistaken."

"You almost certainly weren't. Listen, this isn't an easy decision, but I'm going to be leaving the country. This hotel, it's not safe anymore."

"Where are you going to go?" Tim felt a sinking feeling in his stomach, selfishly thinking about the Imagination Box.

"I would be safer—it would be better for the device—if I continued my research in Germany. Yes. I have friends there, fellow physicists. I will be deconstructing the machine. I will remake the prototype over there. Much better."

Wrapped in both sadness and fear, Tim sighed.

"I will be back, and I will indeed, of course, be in contact. Remember, you're the only person who has been able to make this thing work. You and my invention, well, indeed, you belong together."

"Will I be all right?" Tim asked. "Do these people know about me?"

Eisenstone gradually shook his head, faster and faster. "No, no," he said. "Even if they've seen us together, there would be no reason to suspect you were behind any success. I know this is hard, but what I'm really trying to say is—"

"What do clouds actually want?" Phil asked. Tim turned to see the monkey looking pensively out the window.

"Tim," Eisenstone whispered, drawing his attention back, "listen, you *must* keep Phil secret. You hear me? It's crucial. Crucial indeed. I don't want to scare you, but you really can't trust anyone. I mean that. Remember it. Don't trust *anyone*."

"I understand," Tim said.

"We'll do our final tests tomorrow morning. This is a minor setback in a grand journey, Tim. You understand? This machine isn't merely a bottomless toy box. When it's refined, when it's properly understood, it is going to be a revolution. Imagine, one in every home—what that would mean for those in need . . . commerce, industry, medicine, entertainment. There's no part of society this gadget won't affect."

Tim hadn't considered it before, but the professor was right. The box wasn't just a toy. It was so much more than that.

"We'll get there," Eisenstone added. "Whatever it takes. But you've got to keep what we've been doing quiet. I know it'll be tempting to tell all your friends, but you mustn't."

"All my friends already know," he replied.

There were a few seconds of silence, and the professor smiled strangely, as though he was both happy and sad simultaneously.

That night, in bed, Tim stared for hours at a small sliver of paint in the corner of his ceiling. When, finally, he fell asleep, he returned to a nightmare he'd had countless times when he was small. He was always in his most recent home, completely alone, walking up stairs. But it never ended; the steps just went on and on and on. And then, at some point, he'd hear a sound—something behind, chasing him up the infinite staircase.

The dream always ended the same way. The shadowy, formless beast would gain on him, the ground would become thick—as though he were running through molasses—he'd turn to face his pursuer, and he'd wake just before the creature pounced.

Gasping, lifting his head from his pillow, he realized he was safe in his room. It was what Eisenstone had said, he told himself, about being followed, about being in danger. That was why he'd had the nightmare again. For the first time in a long time, Tim was scared.

CHAPTER 7

In their final morning of testing at the lab, Tim created a number of items. He struggled a little with a few of them, but once he properly focused, he was eventually able to make everything asked of him. And each time, Eisenstone seemed more impressed than the last.

"Amazing. Incredible. Extraordinary," he'd say as he flicked open the lid.

Phil too was taken aback by what he was seeing. All the creations—some hydrogen, a piece of coal, some water—were perfect successes, except one. Tim was asked to make an iron nail. As he was imagining it, he heard a seagull squawk outside the window, and before he knew it, he was thinking about the beach.

When they opened the lid, there was a lump of what could be, and indeed was, described as "disgusting gloop." It looked like green honey, but it had little patches of sand and tiny plants a bit like seaweed. Also it smelled like vinegar and cotton candy. Most unpleasant. This mishmash of thoughts was a stark example of how important it was for Tim to stay focused on the object he wished to create.

Just before lunchtime, Eisenstone lowered sheets of notes and various documents into a shredder, making a curly mass of white paper. He deleted all his records from the computer, and pulled stacks of CDs and tapes off his shelf and rammed them into his case.

After his frantic packing for his flight to Germany, which was the following afternoon, he turned to the desk where the Imagination Box stood proudly in the center, the reader, wrapped in its wire, placed on top. The final item.

"It's going to be sad to say goodbye," the professor said.

"I know." Tim wasn't sure if he was talking to the box or to the professor, or to both.

"Right, indeed, all right, wait here, I'll be five minutes, I need to get some tools to . . . dismantle it," he said, and sighed.

Eisenstone left the room, leaving Tim and Phil by themselves. For a few seconds they both stared at the machine in silence, Tim listening only to his thoughts and the ticking of the clock.

"So," the monkey said, pacing along the desk, "why not make something? Might be your last chance."

"Yes," Tim said, standing, placing the reader on his head. "Great minds think alike."

"Might I submit chocolate as a possible choice?"

"No, I'm not going to make chocolate. We can get chocolate at home."

"Just a bit, just make a *little bit* of chocolate."

"Phil, if I were going to make chocolate, I'd make a lot. But it'd be a wasted opportunity."

"Fine," Phil huffed.

"I think . . . I think I know what to create," Tim said.

Stepping forward, eyes shut, he took a long breath in. His hand hovered above the round green button. Nodding to himself a final time, he knew exactly what he wanted. It was the only logical thing he could make. And, if he was honest with himself, he was actually surprised he hadn't thought of doing it before. It seemed so obvious. Bending the end of his index finger back, whitening his knuckle, he pressed the button with firm certainty.

The beep followed by the cacophony of sound and commotion as the machine burst into life was now completely familiar to Tim. Stepping back, he shared a smile with Phil. The machine rumbled and jigged around, constructing his final thought.

"What did you go for?" the monkey asked.

"You'll see." Tim took the reader helmet off his head and placed it on the table.

They both watched as the device fizzled to a stop and the blinking light returned.

It was done.

When Tim opened the lid, the first thing that greeted his eyes was a large black question mark printed on the side of his creation, which filled the box. Joy danced through Tim's entire being as a drumroll thumped eagerly in his head. It had worked.

"I've done what the genie forbids," Tim whispered.

"Ah, of course you have," Phil said. "Forgive me, but what does the genie forbid?"

"I've wished . . . for more wishes," Tim said, lifting the cube out. "I have created my very own Imagination Box."

"Well, I say, that is terrifically clever, Timothy. Top drawer."

Tim held up a slightly smaller, curvier version of the original. It looked neater and altogether more finished, packaged in sleek silver metal—modern and simple.

Tim reached out and ran his hand across the smooth surface. He found the switch for the hatch right where he had imagined it would be. It took only the lightest of touches, and the top slid back in a far cooler way than the original model's lid. It was like a futuristic automatic door, silently opening and folding neatly away. A complicated mechanism, the workings of which Tim did not even consciously understand, must have been hidden somewhere in the walls of the box.

From inside Tim carefully pulled out a normal-looking black beanie hat.

"Wireless," he muttered to himself, realizing he could remotely use the box and no one would know he was doing so. He turned the hat over in his hands, stretching the material a little, examining it.

Brushing his hair flat, he slowly lowered the beanie onto his head, then put the new Imagination Box into an old backpack they found in one of the cupboards. He smiled at himself in the mirror, with his black hat, his red-checkered shirt, and his new favorite gadget in the bag slung over his shoulders. With a nod, he tightened the straps.

"Looking good, sir," Phil said.

The professor's footsteps approached the lab, so Tim whipped the hat from his head and stuffed it into his back pocket, feeling guilty.

When Eisenstone returned, he quickly got to work unscrewing the bolts and unplugging all the components from his prototype. He was so preoccupied with packing, he didn't even notice that Tim had the backpack hanging from his shoulders.

Tim was almost certain that the professor wouldn't want

him to have his own Imagination Box, but Tim couldn't just let go of the greatest toy in the world. Besides, he could keep a secret, and, really, who would suspect a ten-year-old boy of possessing such a thing?

"Time to go." Eisenstone held the door open as Tim gathered up the remainder of his things. He paused for one last look at the room, all lit up, full of so many different contraptions and components—the accumulation of so much work.

"Ready," he said, turning his back on the lab.

The lights snapped off, and the door slowly hissed shut with a final clunk that quietly echoed down the hallway.

"Here," the professor said when they were back at the Dawn Star, in the corridor between their rooms. "This is where I'm going to be working, in Germany." He gave Tim a business card, which Tim slid into his shirt pocket. "My flight is tomorrow afternoon. I'll see you in the morning. We'll say goodbye properly then."

After he'd said good night, Tim pretty much dived into his bedroom. He'd been shaking with anticipation in the car on the way back to the hotel, desperate to try what he'd made. He removed his Imagination Box from the bag and placed it right in the center of his bedside table, paying careful attention to its positioning. The hat felt snug on his head, and as he took a step away, Phil keenly watched from the bed.

"Ready?"

"Let us proceed," the monkey replied. "In the interest of discretion, I suggest we keep quiet."

"Okay," Tim said, wiggling the fabric reader a little.

He closed his eyes and tilted his head, imagining deeply.

The machine hummed, and he marveled at how much quicker and quieter it was than the prototype. The lid slid open, and Tim pulled out a brand-new set of pencils, ten shades of every color of the rainbow.

He made all sorts of stuff: silly sunglasses; cool sunglasses; a shoe; a tiny little chair for Phil; for some reason, nail polish; a few bags of cotton candy; a treasure map ("We must remember to follow that," Tim said, throwing it down onto the pile); a packet of cheese-and-vinegar chips; a tiny little bed for Phil; a pocket book all about lesser-known camel facts ("Asian camels have two humps, and Arabian camels have just one," Tim read); a tiny little unicycle for Phil; some glow-in-the-dark toy ants; a tomato-flavored strawberry; vice versa; a six-and-a-half-pound note; the other shoe—

Tim stopped and stroked his chin, dropping the final item onto the ground behind him.

"What's on your mind?" Phil asked.

"Well, all this stuff is great and all, but I can't help thinking . . ."

"Oh yes, thinking is essential."

"No, I mean, I just wonder what it *can't* make."

Tim remembered some of Eisenstone's examples as he closed his eyes and tested the limits. This time the Imagination Box seemed to strain. It rumbled along the nightstand, wiggling side to side, constructing his thought. After a few seconds, he stepped forward and opened the lid.

"Ha."

"What is it?" Phil asked.

"Water." Tim frowned, tilting the box and swirling the liquid. "I tried to make hot ice. And I got . . . water."

"Well, to me that makes perfect sense."

But somehow Tim felt he had failed. This wasn't what he'd pictured. "Yeah, but I imagined ice in the shape of fire. It was so clear. So vivid."

"Maybe it melted?"

It was a strange feeling having the box "disobey" him—it was as though he had been overruled by a higher authority. Reality can be a real spoilsport. He thought of the accidental seaside sludge and wondered what other mistakes the box might conjure up, what other ways it could shine a light onto the imperfections of his mind.

After his frenzy of creation, Tim hid as much as he could fit into his closet. Then he put the box inside his backpack and under his bed, before collapsing on top, fully clothed and still wearing his reader hat. It had been fun, but he still felt an emptiness about Eisenstone's leaving (made worse by the fact that Tim had done all *this* behind his back). He knew that at some point everyone leaves, but he'd never expected the professor's departure from his life to affect him quite as much as it was. It was silly, really. He'd known the professor for only a matter of days—and yet. His eyes fixed once again on a flake of paint peeling in the corner of his ceiling. The sound of the hotel's pipes digesting under his floorboards was usually comforting, but not tonight.

Troubled, but snug in his new reader hat, Tim drifted away from reality and into a dark place. His nightmare started as it always did. He was home alone, now in the Dawn Star, at the foot of the infinite staircase . . . and *something* was hot on his heels.

It was early in the morning, and he woke with a gasp. His head was hot, sweaty from the beanie. He pulled it off and dropped it onto his bedside table. The memory of his dream made him shudder as he swung his legs out and stood up. It felt somehow more real than the previous one.

Stepping out of his bedroom to head for breakfast, he felt another wave of doubt about creating his own Imagination Box in secret. Perhaps it would be better to tell the professor. Perhaps he'd—

Tim stopped in the hallway. Room nineteen's door was

wide open, and inside, the hotel's head chambermaid, Mary, was changing the bedding.

"Where is . . . Where's Eisenstone?" Tim thought aloud, peering around.

Mary frowned, then lifted up the corner of the sheet to look under. This was clearly meant to be funny, but Tim didn't even twitch a smile. "Gone," she said. "Left hours ago." She finished routinely tucking everything in too tight, then pushed her cart past him.

The professor had gone without saying goodbye— how could he have done that? No. Something wasn't right. Eisenstone wouldn't just leave, not like that. He wouldn't—

But right then Tim's thoughts were interrupted by an almighty screech from somewhere in the building. A woman screaming, again and again, more and more loudly.

CHAPTER 8

Through room nineteen's window, Tim saw a flurry of feathers fall from the Dawn Star Hotel's gutters as pigeons erupted into the sky, startled by the screaming inside. Another loud, bloodcurdling yell made it easy for him to follow the sound. Without thinking, Tim overtook the chambermaid and headed for the stairs. The terrible noise was coming from the ground floor.

Tim arrived to find Elisa and Donald, the new consultant, already there at room four. The new chef, Stephen, peered through the lobby's oak doors, and guests were beginning to come out of their rooms.

"What's going on?" Tim asked.

"We're not sure. Go back upstairs," Elisa said. She banged on the door to room four. "Is everything all right in there?"

The door swung open. A woman ran into the hallway, clutching her hair.

"Are you all right?" Elisa asked. "What's wrong?"

"There's an animal in there. A monster! A thing. I don't know what it is!" Her fear had now turned to anger. "It's gone back into the vents. I want you to know that I am suing!"

Elisa and Donald entered the room. Tim went in behind them, looking straight to the vent near the floor. The metal grille that opened up to the hotel's ventilation system was damaged. The slats had been bent, snapped, twisted open, and a large hole made in the center. It would have taken a lot of force.

Tim turned, thinking, fearing, realizing. He felt dizzy, sick. Was this still a nightmare? He clenched his teeth. Wake up, wake up, he thought.

He ran straight back upstairs. Rushing, he didn't even see Mary's cart parked outside his room, and collided with it, sending all her cleaning bottles, cloths, and collected towels across the carpet. Too panicked to pick it all up, he burst into his room and slammed the door behind him.

Instantly he swooped to the corner, where, near the

baseboard, the brass slats of the ventilation grille were broken—just like the ones in room four.

"Timothy," Phil said from the bedside table, "what is happening?"

Tim scanned the floor, the walls, even the ceiling. His hands were shaking as he knelt down and pushed his shoulder under his bed frame to pull out the backpack that housed his Imagination Box. His fingers passed over the frayed threads. It had been torn, ripped open—the zipper still intact.

"Oh no," he said to himself. "It's . . . it's real."

"What is?" Phil asked.

Tim didn't answer. He just grabbed a stack of books and rammed them against the vent. Then he got a chair and wedged it between the barricade and his chest of drawers.

"Has something gotten into your room?"

"Worse," Tim said. "Something's gotten *out*. I . . . I fell asleep with the reader on, my reader hat," he explained. "I think . . . I think I might have accidently created my own worst nightmare."

"Well, fiddle my sticks!" Phil exclaimed. "This sounds far from ideal."

Tim's heart was thudding in his chest. Each beat was like being punched—he felt it in his mouth. "I used to have this nightmare, when I was little," he said, staring at the wall. "I was home, alone, and I was running up the stairs. I was being chased by something. By a . . . a monster."

The monkey, who'd clambered onto the bed, glanced over his shoulder, unsettled by Tim's distress.

"It's like . . . I always wake up before it gets me." Tim tried to picture it in his mind. The image was unclear. He couldn't put his finger on exactly what it looked like, or what made it so terrifying. "It's never . . . It's made of shadows. It's a blur."

He couldn't really describe in words what it was. It was more of a feeling—of dread, hopelessness, loneliness.

"Basically," Tim sighed, "it's not a good thing. Maybe Eisenstone was right. Maybe this is what he meant about the possible dangers, what the Imagination Box could do in the wrong hands."

"Right," Phil replied. "And this thing, it is loose in the hotel?"

"Yes," Tim said. "It is loose in the hotel."

Sitting against the wall, with his knees pulled to his chest, Tim managed to calm himself. A minute or so later, outside his door, Mary shouted what he assumed was a Spanish swearword. She'd obviously just discovered that he'd knocked over her cart when he'd rushed back to his room. He pushed himself to his feet.

73

"Mary," Tim said, stepping into the hall, "I'm sorry. I didn't see it."

"It's okay," she replied. "These things, they happen."

She was on her hands and knees, retrieving everything. Feeling responsible, Tim was about to help her. But on the carpet, among all the bleach bottles and cleaning cloths, he spotted something. Something that somehow made him completely forget about the monster he'd accidentally created. The minute hand froze. Time stopped. Staring, fixated on the item that Mary had obviously found in room nineteen, Tim felt his shallow breaths stutter.

Swallowing, he reached down and placed his hand on top of the silver watch. He slowly lifted it and turned it to look on the underside.

The letters P and E were carved on the back, engraved in a delicate font.

CHAPTER 9

Tim wasn't at all surprised when the call to Eisenstone's cell phone went straight to voice mail. He dropped his bedroom phone down with a clunk and sat, illuminated by his lamp, staring down at the old pocket watch.

"Timothy," Phil said, running up Tim's trousers, his lap, and then onto his desk. He sat on top of the watch, oblivious to its importance. "That thing, that yellow thing, the nabina, banboba, branoony?"

"Banana."

"Yes, that, the banana, it was most lovely. It felt right, eating it, if you can comprehend such a notion. It just felt somehow right."

The banana Tim had left for Phil on the desk was covered in tiny bite holes; he'd clearly enjoyed it.

"You are a monkey. That's what you eat."

"Well, it was delightful, and I thank you for it."

Tim's gaze rested on nowhere. "Peter Eisenstone . . . It was his father's watch," he said, thinking aloud.

"Yes, an excellent observation, Timothy. Well done," Phil replied, clearly still daydreaming about bananas. "Wait, what?"

"The watch. It belonged to Eisenstone's father."

"Which watch? Hehe, that is a pleasure to pronounce. Which watch?"

"His watch. His silver pocket watch."

"I am terribly afraid I am not familiar with it."

"Phil, you're sitting on it."

He cocked his head, looking down at his seat. "Ah, yes. Of course. Eisenstone's watch. I conclude that he left it here."

"Yeah. And still no sign of him."

"Okay. . . . Is this a problem? I appear to be missing something." The banana caught Phil's eye. He scuttled across the desk, his claws tapping on the wood all the way to the fruit. He began tugging handfuls out and shoveling them into his mouth. "People do change their plans, it's not unheard of. Oh, whiskers on biscuits," he exclaimed, "this is just so delicious!"

"Eisenstone specifically said he never, ever goes anywhere without it. I know I have an overactive imagination. I *know* that. But . . . but something still doesn't feel right. He wouldn't leave without saying goodbye, and he certainly wouldn't leave his watch."

Phil turned his head farther round than a person could, his mouth covered in glistening food. "So, something has gone wrong? Or maybe he just forgot it. It is a mystery. Who knows? Timothy, how about I sit here and politely wait while you go and get me some cake."

"What? No."

"I see. A reasonable response. So, about this watch, what is the situation?"

"He said he may have been in danger. And he said that he would never be apart from his watch. But he clearly is. That's all we know for sure. So he plans to go to Germany because he was scared. What if he doesn't get there? His cell phone is off, and there's no other way to get through to him."

"I suggest you simply wait for his call," Phil said, and shrugged.

"That's not good advice. I can't sit here doing nothing."

"If you knew where he was meant to be, you could just ring and ask if he is there, then ask about the watch. That, my good friend, would be problem solved."

"But that's the whole thing. I don't know—" Tim

stopped. "The card. He gave me a business card with the lab's name on it. The German lab."

He shoved his swivel chair back and went straight to his closet, slid his shirts left and then right, looking for the one he'd been wearing the night before.

"It's not here," Tim said, sighing. "I might have put it in the laundry basket."

"Why do you not simply *imagine* a new card into existence?"

"I did look at it, so perhaps the details are in my brain somewhere."

It worked. Tim successfully re-created the business card. "Now we have to wait until the professor arrives in Germany."

"So we have some time for cake?"

"Yes, I suppose we do."

Tim punched in the number on his phone. A chirpy man answered.

"*Guten Tag.* Webster-Jones, Inc."

"Um. Yes. Hello. I am looking to speak with Eisenstone, Professor George Eisenstone. He's my . . . grandfather." Tim shrugged at Phil. "Have I got the right number?"

"Hang on. I'll put you through."

There was a long dial tone, followed by a clunk, and then someone else picked up the line.

"Hello!"

"Hello, yes, may I speak to George Eisenstone? Professor. He's English. He's working there. I'm his . . . grandson." He figured it would make more sense if they thought he was family, instead of a neurotic child with an overdeveloped imagination.

"Ah, I am afraid not. You're right. He was *supposed* to be here. In fact, he and I were supposed to be working together this month. I *just* this moment returned from the airport. He didn't arrive."

"You haven't heard from him at all?"

"Not a peep. He called me out of the blue earlier in the week, saying he needed to get away. Perhaps he changed his mind. Perhaps he decided to stay with his family there? His daughter lives quite close to him, as you know. She's your mother, yes?"

"What?" Tim asked.

"Sarah Eisenstone?"

"Who?"

"Your mother. George's daughter . . . You said he was your grandfather?"

Tim's eyes widened.

"No. Yes. I am. Yes. My mother. His daughter. It makes sense, doesn't it? What with me being his grandson. That's how families work."

"To be honest, I thought he had only a granddaughter, but you're clearly a boy."

Tim quickly considered putting on a high voice and pretending to be a girl, but decided it was probably better to continue down his original path of lies.

"Nope," Tim said. "Granddad has only me. No granddaughters at all."

"Must have misheard. Well, I can tell you, I saw everyone else get off that flight, and he was not on it. I am sure he has his reasons. It is possible he's had some kind of brain wave and has locked himself away at his home to work on something incredible. He has done this in the past. The man is a workaholic. When you see him, tell him Benjamin is not so happy."

"Will do."

"Goodbye, young man."

The phone stayed against Tim's ear. The line hummed for a few seconds and then cut to silence.

Perhaps the professor didn't escape soon enough, Tim thought, or perhaps there *was* an innocent explanation. Maybe Benjamin was right—maybe Eisenstone had simply retreated to his home to work. But . . . the watch.

"He never made it to Germany."

"Then," Phil said, "let us find him."

Tim paced across the hotel lobby, waiting for his moment. He had concluded that, in light of Benjamin's comments, the best place to start, as with most possible missing person's cases, was at the professor's home.

When the young hotel receptionist left her post and walked into the office behind to do some photocopying, Tim sat on the counter and swung his legs over. He went straight to the computer, checking over his shoulder to make sure she wasn't looking. After clicking the "Guest Logs" icon, he was presented with a huge spreadsheet. A quick search, typing "Eise," and the professor's details zipped to the top. After jotting down the address, Tim closed the file, stood, and rolled over the wooden counter again. He landed smoothly just as the receptionist returned. She smiled at him, completely oblivious.

As he passed back through the lobby, Tim spotted Donald Pinkman, dressed smartly, sitting on one of the tables, filling out some paperwork. The consultant had a large bald spot and a slender frame. His thin legs were crossed, almost wrapped entirely around one another.

"Ah, Tim," he said, waving him over with a smile. "Come and sit down—have some tea."

Reluctantly, Tim stepped to the table and sat. He would rather have carried on with his investigation, but Donald seemed insistent.

"I wanted to talk to you about the Dawn Star," he said, pouring the tea, the pot's china lid clinking as he set it down. "As you know, as consultant, it is my job to make things run a little more smoothly here. Terrible business with the incident in room four. I shudder to think what kind of vermin could be on the loose. Anyway, I understand sometimes you like to explore—go places you ought not." His tone was like that of a teacher, speaking down to Tim. Speaking sternly. Almost rudely, Tim thought.

"Well," he replied. "This *is* my home."

"Of course," Donald said, his voice overly gentle, patronizing. He smiled just with his mouth, his eyes remaining still. "I understand that. But you must appreciate that this is a functioning business. It isn't professional to have a child running around. *Stealing.*"

Right then, Tim decided he didn't like Donald. What Tim did or didn't do at the hotel was between him and Elisa, he thought.

"Yeah," Tim said. "I'll keep that in mind."

"Oh, I wouldn't want you to take it to heart. You must not feel . . . like a prisoner in your own home. I just think it would pay for you to *keep your nose out of other people's business.*" Donald maintained eye contact, almost daring Tim to say something defiant. But despite the significant temptation, Tim remained polite.

"You're right," Tim said. "I will do my best not to interfere with the running of the hotel."

There was a long pause. Donald narrowed his eyes, as if waiting for a punch line. "Good," he finally said, assuming his warning had worked. "Anyway, enough about that. Your mother told me you're a keen artist."

"That's highly unlikely," Tim replied.

"Oh? Why's that?" Donald asked, slurping his tea. All his limbs seemed a little too long, his large foot swinging as he spoke.

"Elisa isn't my mother," he replied.

"She isn't?"

"No, I'm adopted. Anyway, I've got—"

"I also wanted to talk to you about Professor Eisenstone."

"Really, why?" Tim snapped, then coughed and calmed a little, realizing he might have sounded too eager. "Why?"

"Oh . . . no reason." Donald ran his long finger around the rim of his mug. "The man fascinates me. Elisa tells me you've helped him with his latest work. Judging by his field—nanotechnology, quantum physics—it must have been an amazing opportunity. What did you get to do?"

The lie Eisenstone had suggested came to Tim quickly, like a reflex. "He's been doing a study on children. It's a reading study. I had to read. He's researching how children learn."

"You don't say. That sounds exciting." Donald's eyes—so brown that they were black—widened.

"Nah. There was nothing exciting about all that work.

It was dull, if anything. Dull and boring," Tim said. The professor's words echoed in his head. Their work had to be a secret, just for now.

Donald squinted, and Tim got a strange feeling that Donald was scrutinizing him a little too closely, analyzing every aspect of his face—looking for the lie he'd just told. It must just be his guilty conscience, though, Tim told himself. There was no reason for Donald to suspect anything. Nervously, Tim shuffled in his seat. The prolonged staring made him feel uneasy.

"Anyway. Enjoy the tea," Tim said as he stood and picked up one of the chocolate cookies from the table.

"Remember what I said. I've got my eye on you, Mr. Hart."

"Um . . . ," Tim replied, thinking it a strange thing to say. "Thank you."

He didn't turn back but felt that unbroken gaze following him all the way to the broad oak doors that led to the lava hallway. What a weirdo, Tim thought, arriving at his bedroom.

"Phil?" he whispered, stepping inside. "Where are you?"

A low groan came from his desk as a paper cup and a couple of pencils rolled across the wood, revealing Phil, curled up. Another long moaning sound arose from the tiny monkey, clutching his golf-ball-sized belly.

"Oh, Timothy, help me. . . . I am in jolly big trouble."

"What's wrong?" Tim ran to his desk, terrified, and flicked on his lamp.

Leaning just his head, unable to move otherwise, Phil motioned at an empty glass bowl that had once contained a Dawn Star chocolate fudge dessert. Now it just had brown marks with tiny tracks where he'd clawed out every last bit of cake. With Stephen Crowfield in the kitchen— someone nice enough to turn a blind eye—there had been a steady supply.

"Where's it gone?" Tim asked, lifting the bowl and searching behind his mug full of pens. Phil just shook his head and looked down at himself.

"No," Tim said. "Impossible."

"I thought that too, Timothy. I thought there was no way that amount of cake could possibly fit into such a tiny little monkey. But, alas, it has happened. It is now past tense. It has been committed to reality—there is no room for speculation. All that cake *can* fit into a tiny little monkey. But at what cost, Timothy? *At what cost?*"

"You're just full up. You'll be fine. Now, I think we should—"

"No, Tim, *no*. You do not understand. . . . So much . . . so much cake. It is quite a big portion for a human, but for me?"

"I brought you a chocolate cookie from downstairs, but I suppose you don't want it now," Tim said.

"Well, come along, slow down a minute, Timothy."

Phil pulled himself to his feet, like a fat, drunk cowboy. "I never said I didn't want it. I need fuel for our investigation."

"True. I managed to find Eisenstone's address."

"Well, as they say, it is seldom dandy to dawdle," the monkey said, approaching the cookie. "Let us venture onward."

CHAPTER 10

The bus stopped with a hiss in front of a picturesque house with white-painted bricks and a neat picket fence. A gentle breeze rocked an apple tree slowly from side to side in a nearby garden, leaves rustling. Tim, dressed in his red-checkered shirt, wearing his reader hat, and carrying his Imagination Box in his backpack, looked up and down the quiet street and then set off walking, counting the numbers on the houses. Six, eight, ten, twelve.

Tim still felt a little guilty about the bus ticket. He had been short of cash, but luckily he'd "remembered" he had a pound coin in his bag. This was, no matter how you measured it, a crime. You simply are not allowed to pay for things with fake money. That's an actual law. Even though the coin was indistinguishable from real money, it was still counterfeit. Tim's only comfort was that, even if he confessed, no one would believe he'd imagined the coin into existence.

This wasn't his only breach of the rules that day as, instead of trying to explain the situation to Elisa, he'd told her he was nipping briefly to the shop at the end of the street. Far simpler this way, he'd concluded.

After a short walk, he arrived at number eighteen, Eisenstone's house. There was no answer when he rang the doorbell, as he'd feared. Benjamin had suggested on the phone that the professor might have returned home, to his office, to work on something. Tim, knowing what he knew, had found that to be quite unlikely. Still, he was following the lead, as he had to be sure—had to see for himself. Or, rather, his monkey had to.

"Phil, you're up," Tim said to his pocket, glancing quickly over his shoulder.

"Right you are," the monkey replied, poking his head out, blinking in the afternoon sun.

"Remember, find his office. You're looking for anything out of the ordinary. Has Eisenstone returned home at any point? Any clues at all."

The monkey leapt from Tim's pocket and onto his hand. Tim held Phil up to the mail slot, lifting the shiny bronze flap as he had another quick look around. Carefully Phil crawled through the slot, the horizontal metal door snapping shut behind him.

He was inside.

Tim stepped round to the living room window, where he cupped his face and watched the monkey clamber off a mountain of mail, then scurry into the living room. He looked tiny, a mere shadow darting across the carpet.

"Hello?" a small voice said from behind Tim. "Who are you?"

Spinning, Tim saw a girl around his age. After a moment he recognized her from the photo he'd seen in the lab. It was Eisenstone's granddaughter. She had tightly curled blond hair, kept back by a thick purple hair band. Her baggy, blue-and-white polka-dot dress and her hairstyle reminded Tim of someone from the past. A 1940s swing dancer or something similar.

"Oh. Sorry," Tim said, startled. "My name is Timothy Hart. I'm . . . I'm looking for George Eisenstone."

"He's not here," Dee said. "He's away."

"Do you know where he's gone?" Tim asked, testing the water.

"To Germany, on business." Wrong. "I think he'll be back in a few weeks."

For a brief moment Tim felt the urge to tell her the truth, but he knew that would invariably open up a big can of worms, questions the answers to which were explicitly secret.

"You're his granddaughter?" Tim said.

"Yes. Dee. How do you know him?"

"It's . . . a long story."

"Well, I'll let him know you stopped by. Anyway, good to meet you." She tilted her head awkwardly, clearly wanting their interaction to be over so she could go through the door. "I've got to feed Jingles now . . . so . . ." Dee moved toward the door.

Tim frowned. "Sorry, what? Who's Jingles?"

"Jingles? She's granddad's cat."

"What . . . what do you mean?" Tim shook his head.

"Um." Dee seemed confused by the concern. "I don't know if there's a simpler way of saying it. . . . 'He possesses a feline'? Like a dog, but smaller and . . . like . . . a cat."

"Oh no."

"Not a fan?" Dee said, pushing the key into the lock and swinging the door open.

Tim then, without thinking, pushed his way into the house behind her, desperate to make sure Phil was still in one piece.

"Um," she said, stumbling aside. "What are you doing?"

"I . . ." He realized how dodgy he must have looked, barging into the house like that.

Then his eyes locked on Phil, loitering about in the

90

kitchen doorway. Phew. The monkey tried to appear inconspicuous, staring up at the ceiling and whistling.

Behind him, however, suspended in the shadow of the counter, was a pair of glistening green eyes. Slowly the cat flowed out, moving like water, with predatory ease.

"Phil, run!" Tim shouted.

As Dee turned, Jingles was airborne, flying across the kitchen. Phil was bashed across the tiles by swinging claws, and went spinning on his back. He jumped up to his feet and ran.

"Was that a mouse?" Dee yelled.

The monkey barreled into the living room, zigzagging. In a blink the cat darted after him but missed once again, rolling and bashing into the coffee table. Things slipped and bounced off. Dodging the TV remote, Phil zipped across the hallway and leapt toward the stairs, diving through the wooden uprights of the banister.

Jingles, on the other hand, wasn't quite small enough to fit, but followed regardless. After a very ungraceful thud, the cat spiraled to the ground, dazed, before bolting back into the kitchen, seemingly defeated—perhaps even embarrassed.

The whole thing lasted no more than a few seconds. And although he was sure Dee had probably seen Phil clearly, Tim still jumped between Dee and the stairs, blocking her view.

"What was that?" Dee said.

"What was what?"

"That animal on the stairs," she said plainly. "The one right behind you. You're standing in the way of it. If you just step aside, we can see it."

"Oh," Tim said. "*That*. Well. That's my, um, pet mouse. Yep. Little Phil."

She nodded, frowning. "It didn't look like a mouse. And you're quite clearly lying."

Tim coughed awkwardly. "I'm . . . not . . . lying."

"You just did it again," she said, pointing. "Your eyes. You looked up and right when you were talking. You see, up and left means you're accessing a memory. Up and right means you're accessing the creative part of your brain, i.e., lying. Body language. It's incredibly important."

There was a long drawn-out pause while they simply stared at each other. Tim closed his eyes, defeated but strangely pleased to have to share his secret with Dee. "Right," he said. "I did lie. It's not a mouse, but it's complicated. I can't—"

"No, wait," Dee said to herself. "Hang on. It's the other way around. Up and right is memory; up and *left* is lying. So I would have said you were being honest. But then you just said you *were* lying. . . . Soooo. Let's take a little walk down, down, down"—she did a strange dance with each word—"to truth town."

Eisenstone had told Tim he couldn't trust *anyone*, but surely telling Dee, Eisenstone's own granddaughter, wouldn't cause too much trouble. "What's your favorite animal?" Tim asked.

Dee bobbed her head in thought. "I don't know, um, foxes . . . or . . . Are we allowed mythical creatures? Then it's Pegasus probably. Pegasus. What's the plural? Pegasi? Pegasuses? Pegapods? I suppose there can't be a plural, as there was only one. Anyway, them. Horses with wings. Although, I suppose foxes are quite cool. But . . . no wings. . . . Oh. I don't know. I'd need to do a pros and cons list to give a definitive answer. What's *your* favorite animal?"

Tim stepped to the side, exposing Phil standing at their eye level on the stairs. "Finger monkeys."

"That is amazing." Dee leaned in close, astonished. "What's its name?"

"Phil," Tim said.

"Wow. Where . . . where did you get it?"

"Oh, I am fine, by the way, guys," Phil yelled. "I haven't just narrowly avoided getting devoured or anything."

Dee's mouth sprang wide open. She rubbed her eyes, blinking. "Right," she said. "Tell me *exactly* what's going on."

CHAPTER 11

Once Dee heard Phil speak, there was no point in trying to lie. So, in the professor's kitchen, Tim explained everything to her. The box, the sausage, the nightmare, Eisenstone's disappearance—everything. And it felt good. It felt like he'd untied a knot in his stomach.

"Look," she said with a sigh after he'd finished. "I don't know if you've got something wrong with you or what. I don't know what this is, or how you've managed to make that creature speak, but—"

"You don't believe me?"

"My granddad invented a box that creates whatever you imagine?" She laughed. "Of course I don't believe you."

After a while, however, she gave Tim the benefit of the

doubt and allowed him to have a look upstairs in Eisenstone's house. They discovered that his office had been trashed—someone had come in through the window and messily searched the place.

Dee then suggested, perhaps quite rightly, Tim thought, that they call the police. He remembered the officer who'd come to the lab to discuss the stolen briefcase with the professor. "We should call Inspector Kane," he concluded.

Tim returned to the hotel, and later Dee and her mother, Eisenstone's daughter, Sarah, arrived. Inspector Kane came shortly after, wearing his long coat and with his badge on his belt.

The policeman briefly questioned Elisa, and then Sarah, Dee, Kane, and Tim went to the function room, the very place where Tim had met Eisenstone, where it would be quiet. They sat around a small table near the stage, and all had a good look at the professor's watch. Stephen Crowfield brought a tray of tea and cookies from the kitchen, but only Kane had any. He seemed the only one who wasn't too worried to eat. This was the kind of case he handled every day, Tim thought.

"Now, Tim," Kane said, opening his notepad and clicking his pen. "When did you last see George Eisenstone?"

"It was last night."

"I see. And the work you were doing with him? You were helping him at his lab, is that correct?"

Tim's heart thumped. He had a moment of eye contact

with Dee. He didn't know whether he should lie or tell the truth.

"Yes, we were . . . we were . . ."

Sarah interrupted. "My father was working on a learning paper," she said. "It was a study on children, how they read, how they learn."

Tim saw in her eyes that she wasn't lying. This was what Sarah believed. Eisenstone hadn't even told his *own daughter* about his work. That was how secret it was, Tim thought, feeling a wave of pride, like hot tea going down, followed quickly by rumbling panic.

"Yes," Tim said, his hand trembling under the table. "It was just a study on learning."

The lie tasted terrible. He swallowed hard. Eisenstone's warnings about secrecy rattled in his brain once again.

The interview lasted about twenty more minutes. Inspector Kane spoke for a while about his investigation, what he'd be doing over the coming days before Eisenstone was declared "officially" missing.

"There's quite a procedure to go through," he explained, "and nearly always there's a reasonable explanation."

This offered no comfort.

People do just disappear, Tim thought. He knew that well. After all, that was what had happened with his father. There can be an absence of a "reasonable" explanation, or there can be no explanation at all. People just go.

Before the Eisenstones and the inspector left, Kane, Sarah, Elisa, and Donald talked by the front door in the lobby. Once they were all out of earshot, Dee turned her back on them and stood close to Tim.

"We've just lied to a policeman," Dee said. "Certainly a crime. You sure about this?"

"Eisen—your granddad told me not to trust *anyone*. Your mum doesn't even know about his work."

"If you're sure. So, what now?"

"Well," Tim said, "he was staying here because he thought it was safe. Then he goes missing from his room in the middle of the night?"

"What are you saying?"

"It's not safe, is it?" Tim glanced over his shoulder, across the Dawn Star's lobby. "Someone *here* knows something."

After their other guests had gone, Tim asked Elisa if Dee could stay for dinner that evening.

"Why?" she said. "I mean, what will you be doing?"

"Oh, I don't know," Tim said. "Just hanging out, I suppose. Is it all right? It could even be a sleepover?"

"Yes." Elisa smiled, clearly happy about the idea. It was incredibly rare for Tim to have a friend over, after all. "It's fine by me."

Sarah agreed as well, heading home herself, so it was all settled.

It was just after seven o'clock when they finished dinner. Before meeting Dee, Tim had been expecting to investigate on his own, but now he figured Dee could probably be of some use. After all, she knew Eisenstone better than Tim did.

First, however, before they went over all the evidence and their plan, there was one thing to get out of the way.

"Prove it," Dee said, sitting on the edge of his bed.

"Fine. What do you want?" Tim placed his Imagination Box on his nightstand.

"I . . . I actually need a hair band." She removed the one she was wearing, showing Tim the lightened threads that had worn thin. "See."

"All right," he said, straightening the hat. "Color?"

"In the interest of keeping it unique, and therefore eliminating any elements of trickery, I say make it bright blue, with a yellow-and-orange zebra print on the inside, with just a touch of glitter. Throw some polka dots on the outside for good measure."

"Trickery?" Phil asked. He was sitting on the pillow, stroking his chin.

"Yes," Dee said, turning to the monkey. "How can I be sure, unless the hair band is one of a kind? He could have a hundred hair bands up his sleeve. Sleight of hand.

Distraction. There are countless techniques he could use to dupe me."

"Yes," Phil said, nodding. "Quite right. It is important that we employ skepticism in the face of such outlandish claims. I too desire proof."

"Phil, you *are* proof," Tim said.

"Good point, well made."

"I just need to witness it myself," Dee added.

The very moment the box buzzed and started working, Tim could see that Dee believed him completely. He stood back, holding his hands up, allowing her to open the lid and see for herself, just as a magician might. The hair band was exactly as she'd ordered. She checked the inside, then put it behind her ears and pushed it onto her head. For a good few seconds, she stared at a spot on the carpet, lost in thought, and no one spoke.

"So." Phil finally broke the silence. "Who do you suppose would win in a fight between a shark and a bear?"

"Depends entirely on the environment," Tim said.

"Space station," Phil replied.

"Well, that seems unlikely, but I guess—"

"Give me that hat," Dee said.

"What, why?" Tim took a step away, holding it on his head.

"Because I want a go."

"But . . ." Tim frowned. He felt a strange sense of

jealousy. As if Dee were about to read his diary or look through his Internet history. He wanted to tell her to get her own, but that seemed both childish and implausible.

"Come on, hand it over."

Reluctantly he did as she said and passed the reader to her.

"So, I just imagine whatever I want?" The beanie flattened her hair, making it stick out.

"Yes," Tim said. "Just picture it as clearly as possible, and the box will start working."

Scrunching her face, she groaned and grimaced and seemed to be in genuine pain. After a minute or so of this troubling display of failure, Tim cleared his throat. "Are you . . . finished?" he asked.

"Why isn't anything happening?" she asked, pulling the reader off.

"I don't know. Maybe it's because I created it just for me. It's my tailor-made Imagination Box, after all."

"Right. When I see Granddad, I'm going to ask—no, *demand*—that he make me one."

Although he kind of felt sorry for her, Tim couldn't help but smile with relief. That was why he hadn't wanted to let her try, he realized. He'd been scared she'd be able to do it.

"All right, enough playing," Tim said, taking the reader and flinging it onto the bed. "We've got work to do."

The three of them went over all the evidence, brainstorming everything they knew so far.

"So we know that Eisenstone didn't arrive in Germany, at least not on the flight he had tickets for," Tim said. "He's definitely not at his home. Evidence suggests he hasn't been for a while."

"Mmm," the monkey replied.

"You said he was talking about feeling watched . . . stalked," Dee said, pacing. "Is it possible that these people have kidnapped him?"

"Perhaps, I suppose, yes," Tim said. "Outside the lab, a man in a car took pictures of us. The man could have been scouting out Eisenstone's daily routine, plotting an abduction."

"Who was it?"

"I don't know."

"Professor Eisenstone spoke with some degree of concern about his former partner," Phil added. "A connection?"

"Hmm," Tim agreed. "Professor Whitelock. The one who died in a fire a few months back . . . Maybe his death is linked. Maybe whoever stole Whitelock's teleporter and burned his lab has targeted Eisenstone. I suppose that would be the key, to find out who else knows about his work, about the Imagination Box."

"Is there any way we can get back into his lab?" Dee wondered aloud. "To see—"

Something shuffled in the vents. Fear swelled inside Tim.

"What was that?" Dee cried out.

"Oh, there it is again," Tim said, biting his thumbnail and eyeing the stack of books he'd rammed against the grill. "It's that monster I mentioned."

"Sorry." Dee shook her head. "Remind me again, why did you create it?"

"I didn't *mean* to," Tim said. "I used to have this night-mare when I was small. It's silly, really. I'm all alone and something is chasing me up some stairs. And when your grandfather said he was leaving, he got me all worried, and the nightmare came back. Anyway, I fell asleep with the reader on and . . . well, whatever it is that I'm so scared of in the dream, it . . . well . . . it escaped. It was an *accident*."

"Timothy," Phil said, sitting on his desk. "Was I an ac-cident?"

"What? No. I told you before, I thought it would be cool to have a finger monkey."

"Cool? From my research I have concluded that skate-boards are cool, cell phones are cool. Self-aware, talk-ing finger monkeys? Admittedly I am aesthetically quite pleasing." Phil glanced at himself in the mirror. "But am I *cool*?"

"I think you're cool. Little talking monkey," Dee said. "What's not to like?"

Tim had initially been wary of Dee, but her swift ap-proval of his monkey was tipping the balance in her favor.

Another sound came from the grille in the corner of the

room. "Maybe we should do something about that thing, as it is not at all groovy." Phil looked worried.

"Like what?" Tim said.

"Maybe we could put a camera in the vents," he said. Then he hummed, placing his finger on his furry chin. "That way, we could watch on your computer to see if it is on its way."

"That's actually not a bad— Wait. That's it. Phil, you're a genius!" Tim burst into life, grabbing his sneakers and pulling them on. Dee stopped pacing and glanced between them.

"Yes, well observed," Phil replied. "I am . . . What is the cause of all this energy? Timothy, I find this alarming."

"Cameras!" Tim shouted.

"Cameras?" Dee looked to Phil.

"Well, yes, of course." The monkey still looked confused. "Cameras. Cameras."

"Elisa put *more* security cameras in the hotel, didn't she? In the hallways. There's one at the end of the corridor now, right outside my door, where I found Eisenstone's watch."

"They would have recorded what went on that night," Dee said.

"Exactly." Tim held his top pocket open. "Come on, Phil," he said. "Not a peep outside my room, remember. We've got to check that footage."

Within a minute Tim and Dee were upstairs in Elisa

and Chris's rooms. She was cleaning the dishes while he was reading the paper at the table.

"All right, guys," Chris said with a smile. "What's going on? You having fun?"

"Yes," Dee said politely. "Your hotel is very nice."

"Oh, we try," Chris said. "But it's seen some better days. In fact, some animal-control people are coming tomorrow to look at that pest problem. That woman was pretty shaken up. You noticed anything?"

"Nope," Tim said, glancing at Dee.

"Nothing," she added.

"She said she'd seen a *monster* in room four. Probably more likely to be a rat, I think."

"That *is* more likely," Dee said. "Statistically."

"Crossword." Chris clicked his pen a few times. "*R* something, something, *S*, ten letters. To put back together?"

"Reassemble," Tim said instantly.

"Reassemble," Chris repeated, rushing his pen to the paper. "All right. How about this one—"

"Chris, we've got—" Tim started.

"Twelve across. To thoroughly scrutinize for hidden information. Eleven letters."

"Um . . ."

"Something, something, *V, E* . . . unless, of course, six down is wrong, but . . ."

Dee laughed quietly to herself. "Investigate," she said, smiling.

Tim walked round the table and stood behind Elisa in the kitchen. "Hey, do you need any help?" he asked.

Setting down a large, newly cleaned wooden spoon, she wiped her forehead with her wrist. "That's very kind of you, Tim, but I think I have everything under control."

Relieved she didn't say yes, he asked, "Elisa, you know the security cameras? Are they recording all the time?"

She stopped and looked right at him. He quickly started fiddling with a drawer's handle so he didn't look *too* interested in the answer.

"Um, yes," Elisa replied, frowning. "They do record. All the footage is saved on DVDs. It's a very clever system, actually. It records and burns it all. Mr. Pinkman, he's organizing it, and he just boxes up the discs, sorts them by date, and keeps them in the office. That way, if there's a crime, we can just check back."

"Brilliant!"

"Huh? Yes, it is quite good." She glanced at the sink, picked up a bowl, and began scrubbing. "Strange question. Why did you want to know?" But when she looked back, Tim and Dee had already gone.

They were heading down all five flights of stairs, back to the ground floor.

The lobby was quiet. There was only one guest there,

reading a book on the sofa near the windows, and one member of staff at the front desk. Tim and Dee walked straight past the receptionist—she didn't even look up from the computer—into Elisa's office, and Tim closed the door gently behind them. Dee homed in on the box marked "Security DVDs" and pulled it out across the carpet. Remembering the date they were after, Tim flicked through, and arrived at the subsection marked by a piece of handwritten paper, "Floor two, main hall, camera one."

"Have you found it yet?" his pocket whispered.

"Phil, shush. You know the rules. No talking outside my room."

"Noted. But have you found it yet?"

"No. I'm after the night he left, the . . ." Tim fingered through the security discs, systematically noticing every date in its place.

If they could find the right one, he could simply watch it and find out what had actually happened that night— see what time the professor had left and, crucially, if he'd been alone.

He got to where the DVD should have been, and stopped.

"That's weird," Tim whispered.

"What is?" Phil asked. "Talking to a monkey in your pocket? Or something else?"

"It's not . . . It's . . ." Dee frowned.

"It's missing," Tim added. "The DVD of that night is missing, it's gone. All the rest are here, but that one has been taken out."

"What a coincidence," the monkey mused.

"No, Phil, I don't think this is a coincidence."

CHAPTER 12

"So," Dee said the moment they got back to Tim's bedroom. "What do we know about this Donald Pinkman guy?"

"We know he's in charge of the security cameras, for a start," Tim said. "And he's not very nice. But Elisa seems to like him."

"What's his actual job?" Dee asked.

"He's here temporarily, making the hotel run better. He's a 'troubleshooter,' a 'consultant.'"

"A what?"

"Exactly," Tim said. "Nonsense. Not a real job at all."

"Donald Pinkman . . . *Donald*," Dee said. "It's a silly name too."

"I believe it is the name of a popular cartoon duck," Phil added.

"It is," Tim said. "That's true. He was asking me about Eisenstone too, when we had tea. And then he told me to keep my nose out of other people's business."

"Pretty rude, that." Dee was frowning.

"I assumed he meant stealing cakes and mucking about in the hotel. Maybe he meant something else entirely."

"Temporary contract? Slight weirdo?" Dee nodded. "He's sounding like a prime suspect to me."

"I suggest we find this missing DVD," the monkey said.

Humming in agreement, Tim paced.

There had been no further sights of the deformed monster thing that the woman from room four had insisted was in the vents. However, its intermittent breathing in the walls meant Tim was constantly on edge, always slightly distracted. And when it was silent? He would worry about when it'd next make a noise.

"Okay, that's it." Dee tugged the Imagination Box out from under the bed and threw the reader at Tim's chest.

He caught it and then turned to her, confused. "What? You want something else?"

"Make something," she demanded. "Make . . . make a trap. Something. Something that will mean you don't have to think about that thing all day."

A trap, he thought. Not a bad idea. He popped the hat on and did as she'd suggested. Carefully Tim moved the books out of the way and slammed his freshly constructed device against the grille as quickly as he could, not risking leaving the vent open for even a second. The metal contraption covered the vent well and was held in place with magnets.

"There, that should do it," he said, taking a step back. "Good old magnets."

"How does it actually work?" Phil asked, perched on the edge of the bedside table, his tiny feet dangling. The trap looked a little bit like a small pyramid made from metal.

"Inside there is a very clever detection mechanism," Tim explained. "When the monster comes near the room, through the vents, it will activate the trap."

"And then what?" Dee asked.

"When tripped, it squirts out loads of extremely quick-setting foam. This should solve the problem quietly."

"I see," Phil added. "But will that not kill the monster?"

"I sincerely hope so."

"And does this trap have a name?" Phil asked, raising an eyebrow.

"The . . . the Pyramid of Foamy Doom," Tim said.

"Nice." Dee gave him a quick thumbs-up. "Right. It's obvious what we've got to do now, isn't it?"

"It is?"

"Yes, we've got to rifle through Donald Pinkman's things," she said. "This is the logical next step. Do Dawn Star employees have lockers, anything like that?"

"Um." Tim thought. "I don't think so. I've seen him take things from his car, though."

"Let's go."

After Tim had thrown his backpack with the Imagination Box safely stored inside onto his back and put his reader hat on, they headed downstairs.

Outside in the parking lot, Dee and Tim, with Phil stowed away in his pocket, strolled as inconspicuously as they could. The shadow of dusk was approaching, and a few streetlights were already on.

"It's the black one," Tim whispered as they wandered along the line of vehicles. "It's quite new, not sure of the make, though, maybe a Mer— This one." They came to a stop in front of Donald Pinkman's car. "Now what?"

Dee stepped fearlessly forward and tugged on the door handle.

"Whoa," Tim said. "What are you doing?"

"Trying to open his door?"

"Keep it low-key," he said.

"Well, it's locked, anyway." Dee shrugged, pressing her face against the passenger window. "There's nothing in here."

"What about the backseats?" Tim leaned down and

cupped his hands around his eyes, feeling the cold glass. "Oh my."

"Ding-dong!" Phil said, leaning from Tim's pocket and looking inside. "What's this?"

On the backseat was a book. *The Future of Nanotechnology, Physics in a Quantum World* by Professor George Eisenstone and Professor Bernard Whitelock.

"He said he's taken a great interest in Eisenstone's work," Tim said. "Suspicious."

One of the changes Donald had suggested, to make the Dawn Star more profitable, was to sort out the top floor. For a long time that level had just been used for storage. There were never guests, just old rooms filled with mazes of furniture and dust. This meant that Donald spent a lot of his time up there. In fact, he'd commandeered one of the former suites, which he was now using as his office.

The top floors were off-limits to Tim. However, prompted by Dee's enthusiasm and their recent discovery, he had decided to ignore Elisa's ban. They headed to the upper stories. It was now around nine o'clock, and nearly entirely dark outside. Donald Pinkman's makeshift office was at the far end of the hall. They walked in tentatively, Tim flicking on the light. It was impeccably clean. He saw a telephone and a computer on the absurdly polished oak desk, and a neat pile of paperwork next to the keyboard.

"Weirdo indeed," Dee said. "I read somewhere that guilty people are tidy. Makes sense if you think about it."

Looking out the window, Tim could see the lighted lampposts all the way down to the street below. It was strange how small the illuminated cars appeared. He could really appreciate how tall the hotel was.

"Yeah . . . and why would he want to work all by himself, up here?" Tim asked.

"It could be that he prefers solitude," Phil suggested.

"Or that he's just odd," Dee said.

"But if he does have something to do with your granddad's going missing, then why is he still here?" Tim wondered.

"To keep up appearances." Dee shrugged, as though it were obvious. "If he just upped sticks and left, people would definitely suspect something. Anyway, a little less conversation . . ."

"What are we actually hoping to find?" Phil wondered. "Surely, if he did take the DVD, he would have destroyed it?"

"Maybe," she said. "But *maybe* not. And if he has, then we'll need to find something else, something concrete."

The moment Dee grabbed the wooden handle of the desk's top drawer, a door clicked in the hall. Panicked, Tim slammed himself onto the ground and shuffled under the desk.

"Dee," he whispered through clenched teeth. *"Hide."*

113

Just as Donald wandered in, she jumped toward the window and wrapped herself in the curtain. Tim heard Donald step farther inside, then saw his legs appear by the chair. There was a deep sigh as Donald fell into a sitting position. The computer above Tim's head whirred into life, and while it booted up, Donald began drumming with a pen, humming to himself. However, after two beats the pen slipped from his grasp. Tim winced, scrunching his face as the pen landed on the carpet, right by his knee.

"Whoops-a-daisy," Donald said to himself. He pushed his chair back and leaned down slowly to retrieve it, his face just coming into view as—

A loud buzz brought Donald back upright. He answered his cell and, to Tim's relief, stepped away.

"Hello. . . . Yes, not too bad. . . . Can you hear me?" he said. "Yes. That's better. . . . No real news yet. . . . Yes, the police were here earlier today. They interviewed the boy about the disappearance. . . . No. . . . Sorry. It's the signal. Hang on a second." Tim heard Donald leave the room.

"What is happening?" Phil whispered from his pocket.

"Shh."

Dee emerged from the curtain and crouched. "Where has he gone?" she asked.

Tim stood and peered down the hall—just in time to see the door to the roof drift closed.

"We've got to follow him," Dee announced.

"We can't. I'm not allowed up there."

"You are not allowed on the top floor, but, alas, here we are," Phil said.

"Yeah, but I'm really, *really,* not allowed on the roof. I think that rule is actually backed up with reasons. It's dangerous up there."

"Dangerous?" Dee said. "How? Just stay away from the edge."

"I suppose we could."

"We have to," she insisted. "He's talking to someone *right now* about Granddad."

Tim nodded. "Fine," he sighed, shuffling his bag onto his back.

All three of them headed with determination down the hallway toward the staircase to the roof. Tim arrived at the door, grabbed the handle, and cautiously pulled it down. Gently he tugged. It didn't budge.

"It's locked," he said, confused. "He must have locked it."

"Oh. Well, that is the end of that, then," Phil said, instantly defeated.

Dee tapped on Tim's head.

"Good thinking." He closed his eyes and placed his palm on the metal of the lock.

"What is going on now? What are you doing?" Phil asked.

After a few moments of concentrating, Tim swung his bag off his back, opened up the zipper, and pulled open the lid of his Imagination Box. At the bottom of it was a small silver key, with "Roof" printed on it.

For a brief moment all three gazed down into the opening.

"Goodness me," Phil said, leaning his head out of Tim's top pocket. "A key? But you cannot have known the configuration of the lock. This is most amazing."

"Let's not count our chickens."

Tim peered at his creation, lifting it closer to his eye. It was drooping, almost melting, as though it were made of clay.

"What?" He was confused. "That's not how I imagined it."

"Maybe you're just distracted. Chill out. Make another, but this time out of metal," Dee suggested.

"Wish I'd thought of that. . . ." He pocketed the floppy key and tried again. This time he paid careful attention to the image in his mind. The new one was shiny, glistening. He imagined it cool to touch, heavy in the hand.

Tim grabbed the second key and pushed it into the hole. After his first key, he half expected this one not to fit. However, it was as though brand new. The mechanism was clean and smooth. The door swung open. Tim hoisted his backpack on again, and they raced up the steps, opening the door at the top. And a whoosh of fresh air hit them.

"Right, let's be quiet," Tim whispered, stepping outside.

Donald was standing on the far side, his back to them. With haste Tim and Dee sneaked around the side of the roof, beside some large ventilation boxes, to get close enough to eavesdrop. There were no safety rails, nothing but space between them and the ten-story fall.

The sunset across Glassbridge's horizon was glowing pink through orange, making silhouettes of a distant flock of birds. Mere feet away from certain death, Tim didn't pay much attention to the view. He was too busy straining to hear Donald's hushed conversation.

"Yes. Yes," Donald was saying softly into his phone. "Besides all that, things are going very well here. . . . I had a chat with the child. I think he got the message. He runs around like he owns the place."

Dee raised an eyebrow at this, but Tim just kept listening, his ears burning red.

"Oh yeah, that," Donald continued. "God knows what that is—something in the vents, probably vermin. . . . Well, yes, that too. It's not good for business if everyone knows people go missing from this place."

Tim, Dee, and Phil all shared a glance.

"I don't think the police have any leads. Obviously, for

117

my purposes it'd be better if the professor's disappearance was kept *out* of the public eye. Swept under the rug as best as possible. Would be a disaster to have it linked to the Dawn Star or to me. Anyway, I'll keep you posted. Speak soon." He hung up.

As Donald turned around, he looked almost as though he could somehow feel he was being watched. Tim dropped lower in his hiding place. Then the consultant walked slowly to the stairs and back down indoors.

"My God, did you hear that?"

"I heard," Dee said. "He wants to keep the disappearance a *secret*?"

"Yes, Timothy, what now?" Phil asked, his arms and head hanging out from the shirt pocket.

Going over everything again, Tim considered the situation. Eisenstone's watch, the missing DVD, and now this phone call. Was it enough evidence to prove that Donald was involved in whatever had happened to the professor?

He slipped down to sit cross-legged on the cold gravel, his back against the waist-high ventilation box, which throbbed behind him. Dee slouched beside him. Both stared at the last sliver of moon that could now be seen in the sky. After a few seconds Tim felt the fan inside spin to a stop, fading quietly, but he thought nothing of it.

"I think we should tell the police, tell Inspector Kane," he said decisively. "We should pass on everything we know."

So embroiled was he in this new development that he had forgotten about his nightmare monster, loose in the hotel's vents. But it had not forgotten about him. The grotesque creature crawled slowly and purposefully on top of the metal directly above their heads. It watched. It waited.

CHAPTER 13

The beast struggled with six twisted legs the color of long-dead flesh, with thick black hairs protruding out at various angles. There was one ogling eye on the left side of its "face." This monster was truly a creation from the darkest places inside Tim. The makings of a nightmare.

"Without concrete evidence, what will Inspector Kane do, though?" Phil asked.

"I don't know," Tim said, biting his thumb and staring across the roof. "Take Donald in for questioning?"

A long streak of drool trailed out of the animal's mouth, glistening in the warm dusk light.

"That's my vote," Dee said. "We go straight to the police. That's the rational reaction to this. Whatever mess Granddad is in, we've got to sort it out."

"Yes, fine, we'll go and—"

The spit landed on Tim's shoulder and ran down his arm. "What?" Confused, he very slowly turned, desperate not to see what he thought he might.

Inches from his face, the monster hissed. Scrambling to his feet, shaking, Tim shuffled backward.

Dee had yet to notice. She stood up, frowning. "Tim, are you all right?"

Clueless as to what the monster would do, Tim held his hands up. The only thing that saved Tim in his horrible dreams was the realization that it was, in fact, a dream. Here, though, in the real world, he didn't have this safety net. There was no escaping. He could *not* wake up.

The creature leapt onto the ground, sending several pieces of gravel flying as it growled again. Dee's body tensed as she finally turned to look at the creature.

"What is *that*?" she said, stepping back.

Holding itself up to its full height on its stunted legs, it seemed almost proud of the fact that it had joined Tim in the real world, where it could truly terrorize him. Like a rabid dog, snarling and snapping, it advanced. Its joints clicked and squelched as it jerked along.

"Um," Dee said, throwing her arms into the air.

"Suggestions? Tim? What shall I do?" There was no response. "I feel I should kick it, but I don't want to."

Phil's head emerged from Tim's pocket. "Oh, that is just ghastly. What the . . . Good grief."

It occurred to Tim that this was not a perfect model of his dark vision. It was poorly constructed. His having created it during his sleep must somehow have made it worse. He continued to stagger backward as his heart hit the inside of his rib cage, over and over, so hard that he could feel it in his neck.

Scurrying side to side, the creature let out a haunting, throaty gurgle.

"All right, this is a bit much," Dee said. "I'm going to get help." She turned and ran across the roof, back toward the stairs.

There was less than a meter between Tim and the edge of the roof.

"Timothy, stop. The edge!" Phil was now yelling. He climbed from Tim's pocket onto Tim's shoulder, tugging on his collar. "Stop!"

But all Tim could do was retreat. Gripped in the tightest hold by fear, he couldn't think beyond moving away. His heels were now flush with the edge of the building. Tiny pieces of dust and gravel crumbled off the roof, falling fast to the ground, where they disappeared out of sight.

There was a standoff.

"It's . . . stopped. What . . . what does it want?" Tim whimpered.

He finally turned, spotting how close to the edge he was, and as he did so, the monster let out a screech, louder than any before. The sound shook Tim to his core. He swiveled back to the monster, then swayed, losing his balance. His left foot slipped off behind him, followed by the right. Instinctively he threw his weight forward as he fell, catching the gutter with his hands just in time. He was now swaying off the side of the building.

Phil scurried to Tim's hand, where he started nobly pulling on Tim's sleeve, but it proved useless. Tim's fingers scrambled, desperately searching for something else to grab on to. He slipped down a little as the gutter sagged. His legs frantically kicked below him, flailing in the thin air. The monster came near, its breath on his hair, almost making contact. Tim closed his eyes and waited. But the beast turned, cowering, and crawled away, back to its vents. Where was it going? It had Tim at its mercy. Why was it retreating now?

With a deep breath Tim tried to swing himself back up, but the gutter broke. He fell farther—bashing his chin— and was now hanging by just his fingers, with ten floors of nothing below him.

"Tim?" called a voice from above. It was Dee. "Uh, Tim? Where are you?"

"I'm here!" he groaned.

Her head appeared above him, next to Phil, her hair hanging down as she leaned over. "I went to get help, but the door is locked."

Tim could only gasp, and then: "Pull me up."

Dee lay down flat, grabbed his arm, and tugged with what felt like a feeble amount of effort. He barely moved. "You're too heavy."

"No, you're just not strong enough."

"What a pickle," Phil added.

Tim twisted his weight from raw panic, causing a screw to ping off above, and the gutter he was clinging to lowered another foot or so and then bounced to a stop. Now dangling from a vertical, disconnected bit of metal, there was only a single, very rusty bracket keeping him alive.

"I am going to die!" Tim shouted up, his hands sliding, arms burning. "It's as simple as that."

"No!" Dee yelled. "Make something, anything!"

Tim scrunched his face, trying desperately to imagine a way out of this situation, thinking hard over the distracting circumstances, his numb grip now unreliable.

"Come along," Phil yelled. "Faster."

"You know, that doesn't actually help me concentrate."

Tim closed his eyes again. "Done!" he said. "Quickly, climb down the gutter and open the box, Phil."

The monkey leapt onto his shoulder, then onto the bag,

where he tugged the zipper open. "What in heaven's name is this?" he asked, peering into the Imagination Box.

"Pass it to me," Tim ordered. There was no time to explain. He held on to the gutter with his right arm, and waved his left hand about behind him until he felt the fabric in his palm. Hastily he pulled one strap over his left shoulder, then switched hands so that he could pull the other onto his right. The pack rested on top of his backpack, and he snapped the buckle shut round his front.

"Is that a . . . jetpack?" Dee asked in a high-pitched voice.

"Yes. Now, let me just—"

The gutter snapped—they fell—the roof disappearing above.

Tim clawed at his invention, fumbling for the right buttons as he and Phil dropped through the howling air.

In a blink they were nearly at the ground, just as the jetpack erupted—bright, spewing flame and smoke, slowing them, and then lifting them away from the building, wildly spinning.

Tim, for a moment, seemed to have control. They flew awesomely into the air, in grand circles. They were *actually* flying. But then they flew straight into the side of the hotel.

They smashed headfirst into a window a few stories up, before bumping down the bricks, fire and vapor still bellowing out of the contraption. Near the ground they spun upside down, drifting out a bit, before Tim let go.

He landed with a thud, seated and still with his backpack on his back, the Imagination Box intact inside. Phil landed on top of Tim, followed by the jetpack—all strung out on the pavement. After a sputter, the jetpack fired up by itself and spiraled off at great speed along the ground, leaving a foggy trail, before wedging itself under a parked car. The heat blasted from the back of the jetpack for a second, and then it sparked, fizzled, and seemed to stop.

"Ouch," Tim said, glancing around. A new appreciation for solid ground washed over him as he stroked the cold concrete.

He was safe.

"That was . . . stressful," Tim said, coughing. He looked up to see Dee's tiny head. Her hand came out. She waved and gave him a thumbs-up.

"Maybe you should listen to Elisa?" Phil said, clambering onto Tim's chest.

"Yes, I agree, the roof is, quite rightly, off-limits."

"You know, I think Dee meant for you to make a rope, or something of that nature."

"Yeah," Tim croaked, propped up on his elbow. "Maybe, in hindsight, that would have been better, but the jetpack still got us down safely."

"Just."

"And it's an all-right creation, I think, all things considered."

The jetpack exploded under the car, blowing glass and fire onto nearby vehicles. A symphony of alarms kicked off as thick black smoke, filled with fresh embers, rose up into the sky.

Phil's eyes bulged at the surprisingly large flames. "Shall we go indoors?"

"Yes, please."

CHAPTER 14

Tim and Dee got up early to head to the police station. They had toyed with the idea of calling the police the night before, but Eisenstone's warnings about trusting no one had held them back. They needed to speak with Inspector Kane—no one else would do. Tim put everything on: his clothes, hat, and backpack. It had become routine that he'd take the Imagination Box with him wherever he went. In fact, he felt naked without it. The station wasn't far from the hotel. Tim, Dee, and Phil crossed Glassbridge's large park, cut a diagonal path up the busy high street, and arrived within fifteen minutes.

On their way out Tim had told Elisa that they were

going to speak with Inspector Kane about something he had remembered from the night of Eisenstone's disappearance. It was kind of a lie, but kind of true. (They'd decided it was too premature to tell her about what they'd discovered. In fact, Tim imagined she'd tell him to "stop being silly" if he started accusing Donald Pinkman of any wrongdoing.)

"Funnily enough, you just missed the police," Elisa had said. "Someone broke a window and started a fire in the parking lot last night. You must have heard a bang?"

"We were fast asleep," Tim said.

"Like a pair of babies," Dee added. "Drunk ones."

The previous night Tim and Phil had managed to slip into the hotel as people had rushed out to see what all the noise was. They'd gotten upstairs, and Tim had opened the roof door for Dee without anyone spotting him. They had then gone straight to bed. Tim had had his lies poised, his excuses ready.

Luckily, there had been no knock at the door.

The police station's reception area smelled like school—paper, pencils, and faintly warm plastic from the computer. The lady at the desk fetched Inspector Kane, who smiled when he spotted them both.

"Ah, Dee, Tim, come on through," the policeman said. Kane waddled as he walked down the long corridor. The floor was shiny and green, with odd black rubber scuffs on it like on a gym floor. They all arrived in Kane's office, where the inspector checked up and down the corridor before closing the door.

"Please, sit," he said, pointing at a couple of chairs.

Kane moved his body round the desk and sat on his slightly higher swivel chair, directly opposite. "So, what can I do for you today?"

"Well, it's about Professor Eisenstone. Since he went missing, we—"

"There are inquiries being made—he's not been declared missing *officially,* but carry on," Kane said. He picked up his mug of coffee and began taking a swig.

"We think Donald Pinkman might know something about it," Tim said.

Inspector Kane stopped with his cup at his mouth, and took a good couple of seconds before he swallowed his coffee.

"Right." He placed his mug carefully on the coaster. "Why do you think that?"

"He's working at the Dawn Star Hotel," Tim said. "As a consultant, as you know. Anyway, he started not long before Eisenstone went missing."

"I see." Inspector Kane leaned back in his chair and pulled out a notepad from his top drawer.

"And . . . well, we think he might know something about it. I think you should speak to him again," Tim said.

Slowly shaking his head, Kane clicked his pen a few times. "Hmm. What, exactly, are you basing this on? You can't just go round making accusations."

They then explained what they'd discovered—the missing security footage and the fact that Donald had access to the DVDs.

"I'm afraid this is flimsy evidence, Tim, as interesting as it is," Kane answered.

"We heard him talk about Granddad on the telephone." Dee spoke up, tapping the table with her finger. "He mentioned my grandfather by name. He said it would be best if the disappearance was kept quiet."

Inspector Kane sighed. "Well, it would look bad for the Dawn Star, I suppose. I've spoken to Mr. Pinkman. He works for a consultancy firm. He was probably checking in with his organization. Look, people talk about people all the time on the phone. The professor is well-known, he might be missing. There are thousands of reasons why Mr. Pinkman could be speaking about him. We're speaking about him now. Are any of us guilty?"

"And he told me . . . he told me to keep my nose out of other people's . . . business. . . ." Tim deflated. All of a sudden he was full of doubt, wondering whether there could be an innocent explanation for all he'd seen and heard.

"Listen." Kane placed his pen on his pad. "I admire

your enthusiasm, but I fear you are maybe letting your imagination run wild."

Tim couldn't help a smile. "But . . ."

"Okay," Kane said firmly. "It's *our* job to find Professor Eisenstone. If there is any wrongdoing, rest assured, we'll get to the bottom of it."

"I . . . it's just . . ." Tim struggled to find the words. He was annoyed that Inspector Kane wasn't taking his theory more seriously. Perhaps if he knew the importance of the contraption . . .

"His work," Dee said, clearly thinking the same thing. "It was very . . ."

"What do you know about his work?"

Eisenstone's words echoed in Tim's mind. He gave Dee the slightest of head shakes.

"I don't know anything much really," she said. "But he told me it is . . . important."

Kane's interest dispersed, and his chair creaked as he reclined. "I'm sure it is. Now I urge you, as a police officer and as a friend, to stop this. It's not a good idea to carry on snooping around. There is a process, and anything you do could interfere with that."

Tim nodded, but he wasn't really listening. His mind was spinning, possible explanations for his friend's disappearance flashing and bouncing around in his head. He needed answers.

• • •

Initially the meeting with Inspector Kane took the wind out of their sails. But the moment Tim and Dee got back to the hotel, they picked up where they'd left off—looking for harder evidence. They knew they needed something concrete to make the policeman take notice.

Much later, sitting at his desk, a little after three-thirty a.m., Tim rubbed his temples in gentle circles. The lamp made an oasis, a warm yellow bubble in the cold of night where he thought of only one thing: Professor Eisenstone.

Dee had convinced her mum to let her stay another night. They both stared down at Tim's sketch pad. The whole case—all of Tim's notes—was scribbled messily on the paper, bordered by various sketches, some of random patterns and some of Phil. Tim had half drawn a picture of his nightmare monster, but had since scribbled it out. The creature was still at large, still tormenting him from the vents.

Tim and Dee had talked at great length about where to take their investigation next. Both had agreed, and Tim circled the final bullet point: "Eisenstone's former partner."

"Professor Bernard Whitelock," Tim said. "He worked with Eisenstone but died a couple of months back. He helped design the Imagination Box. It seems that

Professor Eisenstone, Professor Whitelock, me, and now you are the only people we can be *sure* have ever known about it. . . . Who is Professor Whitelock?"

"I met him once or twice when I was small," Dee said. "But I know that something happened between them—I think something with their work. Granddad never really spoke about it. Either way, they weren't close toward the end."

They spent the next hour searching the name, and every variation, online. They'd done this before but had only had a cursory glance. Now, though, they decided to dedicate some real time to researching Whitelock. They read some of his papers on nanotechnology, most of which were incredibly technical. There were no clues. Tim found an article in some obscure academic journal about Professor Eisenstone and Professor Whitelock. There was a photo of them both, posing in a lab. Eisenstone didn't look much different, besides having slightly more hair and it being thicker and brown.

The last site they read was an obituary. It was all about Professor Whitelock, his work and his "tragic death." It didn't mention his troubled final years that Eisenstone had spoken of. In fact it just seemed to praise the man as a genius. Tim read the final paragraph, his chin resting on his hand.

"The untimely death of this great man was a shock to

the academic community as much as to friends and family. Professor Bernard Whitelock leaves his wife, whom he married just months prior to his death, former Glassbridge member of parliament Clarice Crowfield. The professor's contribution to scientific advancement is indisputable; his work has paved the way for—"

Bolt upright now, Tim turned to Dee, who leaned closer to the screen. He shook his head and reread the last two sentences.

Their attention, in unison, fell on the name Clarice Crowfield.

Professor Whitelock had married Clarice *Crowfield* before he'd died.

Tim had thought it when he'd first met the new chef, and he thought it once again: Crowfield was not a common name.

CHAPTER 15

"Stephen Crowfield . . . the new chef," Tim said, still sitting at his desk, taking it all in. "This is it. This is the connection."

Dee explained, in her ever-rational way, that more evidence was required. "This could still be a spurious correlation," she said, fist on her bottom lip.

"A whaty what?"

"A spurious correlation is when two things appear to be linked but in fact are not," she said. "It pains me to say it, but Inspector Kane might have had a point. We can't let our imaginations guide us any further. We need to head down to fact town."

She was right. They had to be sure. "What have you got in mind?" he asked.

"Is there a record of when Dawn Star staff work?"

"Um." Tim nodded. "Yeah, there must be. The rotas."

"Where are they? Or, more specifically, where is Stephen's?"

"His will be at the workstation at the back of the kitchen, I imagine."

"We could look at it, find out if he was here on the night before Granddad's flight?"

"Let's go."

Tim hadn't even realized the time until they stepped out of his bedroom. The hotel was dead, silent. Straight down the stairs, through the hall—no time for lava—to the lobby, which was completely empty besides the night porter, who was slumped, reading a magazine at reception. He didn't notice them briskly pass through and to the kitchen doors.

"Down here," Tim said, pointing ahead of them.

It was weird seeing this place—usually bristling with commotion and heat—in a quiet and cold state. Everything seemed gray. At the back of the room, behind a dividing wall, was a messy desk. Tim switched on the lamp, and without another word, Dee began searching through the drawers.

"This it?" she said, holding up a folder.

"Looks like it."

With a lick of her thumb, she flicked through the staff rota, scanning down the column marked "S. Crowfield," noticing the days the young chef had filed overtime. There was just one single evening he'd worked late: the night Professor Eisenstone went missing.

"That's it," Tim said, placing his finger on the entry, then tapping it. "And look. He's not down to work from next week onward."

"Maybe he quit?" Dee wondered. "Maybe his job is done." With that, she returned the folder to the third drawer down. "We should leave it as we found it. We don't want to arouse— Wow. What's this?"

She slid a plastic DVD case out from under some pens and clutter and handed it to Tim. Tim removed the disc and inspected it. Something on the front had been scribbled over with black marker. He flipped it over to see that the back was scratched. There were deep grooves across the rainbow silver.

"This has got to be the footage of that night," Tim said. "Whatever is on here, Stephen doesn't want the world to see."

"Why hasn't he gotten rid of it completely? He's not very good at this, is he?"

"Definitely careless." Tim turned the lamp off and pocketed the DVD. "Even if this is damaged, they can still recover data from these things."

Walking briskly from the kitchen, Dee whispered from behind, "We need to confirm that Stephen and Clarice are definitely related."

"Crowfield is a pretty rare name," Tim said quietly over his shoulder.

"I know, but we've got to be certain."

"How?"

"We could look up his address, his number?" Dee suggested. "We could ring and ask for Clarice."

"That's just—"

"So simple, bold, and logical that it makes complete sense?" Dee smiled. "Why, thank you."

They paused at the edge of the restaurant, before rounding the corner and heading back into reception. "We'll need to look on Elisa's computer," Tim said, peering at the night porter. "Which means getting rid of him."

"Hmm." Dee turned to look at the phone on the wall by their side, used by waitstaff to take reservations for the hotel restaurant. She picked it up. The tone hummed gently. "How do you call reception?"

"Um, press nine and then press the hash key."

She hit the buttons and, still hidden behind the corner, twirled the curly cord as she spoke in a very posh adult voice. "Ah, yes, hello there," she said to the porter. Tim couldn't help but snigger. "My name is Francesca Bumblesnatch. I am staying in room thirty, and I think there's a burst pipe in the hallway. There's a terrific puddle of water. I suggest you come right away."

"Oh, thanks for letting me know. I will check it out," the porter said.

With the porter gone, they swept to the office behind reception and logged on to the computer. Tim clicked on the staff folder on the desktop, opened it up, and took down the chef's home number. He noticed his address was Crowfield House.

Back in his room, Tim had typed "Crowfield House" into his search engine only to find that the home was an old insane asylum. Now, spurred on by Dee, Tim was dialing, not giving a thought to how late it was. After a few rings, a flustered woman answered.

"Yes, hello," she said in an angry, tired voice. "Do you know what time it is?"

"What is your name?" Tim asked. Dee gave him a firm thumbs-up, clearly pleased with how direct he was being.

"*You* rang *me*. You know perfectly well that I am Clarice Crowfield and—"

Tim hung up. "Right," he said. "Stephen lives with Clarice."

"And that was her name when she married Professor Whitelock," Dee said.

"So . . ."

"It's probably her maiden name. So she's not Stephen's wife. Got to be a relative. Sister? Mother?"

"She sounded old."

"Mother, then."

"We need to speak with Inspector Kane," Tim said. "We can't trust anyone else."

"So we've got to wait until the station opens?" Dee shook her head. "No way. Stephen's done *something*. Whatever is on the DVD is obviously incriminating. What if they've taken Granddad? Or worse? Plus, what if Inspector Kane *still* doesn't think this is enough to investigate? You saw how reluctant he was to do anything. He thought we were speaking nonsense."

"Well, what are you suggesting?"

"I think we should go there, to their house, and have a look about," Dee said. "Get some concrete evidence."

"When?" Tim asked. "Now?"

A moment later Dee was zipping up her jacket and slipping on her shoes. Tim tied his laces, stood, and finally placed his reader hat on in front of the mirror. Dressed in a dark shirt, he tightened the straps on his backpack. He was ready.

Tim pulled open the top drawer of his nightstand to see Phil tucked up peacefully in his perfectly made miniature bed. "Phil, wake up," Tim said.

"What in heaven's name? What time is it?" the monkey mumbled.

"I don't know—a million o'clock? We're going out. Do you want to come?"

"Pardon? Where? It is still dark."

"We're going to Crowfield House."

"I beg your pardon, Timothy?"

"We've had some breakthroughs. We need to look in Stephen Crowfield's home." Tim then explained what they had learned.

"You plan to break in?" Phil asked, standing.

"Don't make it sound like *we're* the bad guys," Tim said. "But yes."

"We have just cause, Phil," Dee added. "This is all very reasonable."

She swung her coat's hood onto her head. In the shadow Tim could still see the white polka dots on the hair band he'd made for her.

"What about Elisa?" The monkey was concerned, as Tim knew *he* should have been.

For some reason he just couldn't find anywhere in his head that worried about the consequences of what they were doing. He thought for a moment about the day when he'd met Eisenstone—the stolen cakes. What a tame crime that had been, and now he was preparing to leave in the dead of night to break into someone's house.

"Elisa won't mind," Tim said. "She won't find out."

"Hmm, is this not a trifle . . . illegal?"

"Certainly," Dee said. "But, like, what's the worst that could happen?"

"Prison?" the monkey suggested.

"For breaking into someone's home? No," Dee said. "Children rarely go to prison. Especially not for something minor. I think this kind of thing is frowned upon, sure, but legal consequences? Pfft, unlikely."

"I am afraid I am still a little apprehensive," Phil added.

"Look." Tim sighed. "Clarice Crowfield, who lives with Stephen Crowfield at Crowfield House—an old mental asylum—married *Professor Whitelock*. Remember, Eisenstone's old colleague, who died?"

"Okay. I am following so far."

"I think Clarice Crowfield knows something about the Imagination Box, about Eisenstone's work. First, the fact that the professor left his watch is enough reason to be sure that Eisenstone is missing. We've checked everywhere he should be. He's gone. And now, we've just found the missing security footage with Stephen's things. The fact that Stephen Crowfield has concrete links to the *only* other living soul we can be *sure* knew about Eisenstone's invention, *and* he was working here the very night the professor disappeared . . . Don't you get it, Phil? It all adds up."

"Totally fits together," Dee agreed. "Tim's right. Plus, Inspector Kane won't listen until we have something absolute. We need proof."

"Yes," Tim said. "You took the words right out of my mouth. Now, it could be risky, it could be dangerous. You don't have to join us if you don't want to. I will completely understand if you'd—"

"Worry not, old bean. I am coming."

CHAPTER 16

The first embers of the morning sun were just appearing in the sky, but predawn blueness still covered everything in sight. Tim, Dee, and Phil made short work of the trek across Glassbridge and up Chestnut Hill, to the highest point in town.

Having jogged most of the way, they slowed to a walking pace quite a long distance from their target. Ivy, much of which was dried onto the crumbling bricks, climbed up and over the perimeter wall. The gate had grand, curly fittings at the top, with "Crowfield House" spelled out in fancy writing cast from iron. They stood at the entrance, looked through the bars, and watched the building for a few moments.

There wasn't a single glowing window. This was good news; if everyone was asleep, it would make their break-in easier. There was still no doubt in Tim's mind, no fear, and no suggestions that they should turn back. Some of the gray wall was broken, with some cracked bricks half-way up. Tim found his footing and scrambled up and over. After landing on damp grass on the other side, he stood and wiped his hands on his jeans. It was there he had his first shimmer of worry. Besides making the counterfeit bus fare, this trespass was the first real crime Tim had ever committed. (He decided that the jetpack explosion didn't count because that had been a genuine accident.)

Dee fell behind him, just keeping her balance.

"You . . . you sure about this?" he whispered, swallowing.

"No," Phil said from his pocket.

"Well." She shrugged, brushing herself off. "We've come this far."

The turf was soft underfoot. They made sure not to step with muddied footprints onto the paved path that led up to the driveway and, after a short walk, made it to the side of the house. Tim had planned to quickly create a key, but saw that the back door was boarded up with wood and nails.

"Looks like they're trying to keep people out," Tim said, rubbing his hand across one of the planks.

"Or keep someone *in*," Dee suggested.

Crowfield House was huge, imposing, and, Tim couldn't help but admit, scary. It looked as though it had been abandoned years ago, with overgrown foliage and peeling paintwork. Above them was an open window. On their left was a wooden trellis with crinkled, dead plants clinging on to it. Tim tugged, making sure it was sturdy. When they decided it could safely hold their weight, Dee began climbing and, at the top, passed her legs over the windowsill.

"Shh," she said, helping Tim in.

His vision adjusted to the new light, and, realizing he was in a bedroom, his eyes snapped to the bed. It was empty. They moved silently, but a few steps in, there was an incredibly loud creak from a floorboard beneath the carpet. Sweat prickled up his back as he carefully lifted his foot. As slowly as humanly possible, Dee opened the door and they passed through into the hall. Tim was shaking as they crept through the house, to the stairs, where he saw the grand entrance from the inside. A sudden wash of new panic hit him.

He grabbed Dee by the arm. "What if they've got a dog?" he whispered.

"Then I imagine it'll probably bark in the next few seconds," she said, stepping onto the first step.

The search of the ground floor was fairly quick, and luckily there were no pets to give them away. There was some unusual antique furniture, but none of the concrete evidence they had hoped to find. Until, that is, they arrived in the study.

This was by far the largest room they'd come across. It had floor-to-ceiling bookcases and a wide desk in front of two long windows covered with thick velvet curtains.

The first thing Tim noticed was the huge, imposing painting of a woman on the wall. A small silver plaque at the base read: "Clarice Crowfield." Wearing a posh suit and a thick gold chain, she watched over the study, constantly maintaining eye contact with them wherever they moved. Below, pinned to the wall, there were countless newspaper clippings and photographs. Headlines proclaimed her a "rising star," and black-and-white snapshots showed her shaking hands with important public figures, some of whom were familiar to Tim. He thought it strange that she'd have such a dominant portrait of herself.

"Do you recognize this woman?" Tim asked.

"Nope."

A little farther along, perched on a polished wooden pedestal in the corner, was a stuffed owl that also watched over them, its glassy eyes glistening like this year's pennies.

And then they spotted it.

On large bulletin boards, mounted on a few artists' easels, was a sea of evidence. Although this was what they'd hoped to find, the discovery made Tim's heart sink. The Crowfields were extremely guilty. There were countless photos of Eisenstone, with Post-it notes and arrows linking scribbles to one another. Tim's fear ramped up a gear when he spotted pictures of himself. Some were of him entering the lab with the professor and getting in and out of his car, confirming again what he thought he'd seen. There were notes bordering an early blueprint of the first Imagination Box prototype. It was a detailed sketch that had obviously been stolen. Every part of it was labeled with thick blocks of text.

"Look," Tim whispered.

"They stole all of this," Dee added, lifting her brow. "Cheeky freaks."

"This is enough. Let us go," Phil said.

"No, wait a second." Tim stepped closer to the collage of evidence. "Look, they've got Eisenstone's notes that he was making with me. It says what he'd created. A sausage, a marble, *a finger monkey*—they know everything."

"Really? Oh. We should definitely leave." Phil wriggled in Tim's pocket.

"Check this out," Dee said.

On one of the boards was the date of the professor's flight to Germany, with "Abducting the information" written beneath.

"Wait, can you feel that?" Tim said.

"Feel what?" Phil replied.

"A draft."

They followed the cold air. It brought them to one of the bookcases across from the desk. Dee licked her thumb and held it at the edge of the wood, between two sets of shelves.

"It's coming from here," she said, craning her neck. "This is a door."

With the tips of his fingers Tim tugged at the small gap, trying to get the case to move. It was no use. He stepped back, defeated.

"Maybe not?" Phil said.

"Or perhaps there's a secret button or something?" Tim replied as he started inspecting each shelf. "If they've got all that stuff in plain view, just *imagine* what they'd want to hide."

Dee began pushing loose books around, looking at the shelf behind them, but one of them didn't budge—it was fixed. Tim and Dee shared a smile.

Slowly she pulled the book down toward them. A low clunk followed by a hiss, and the set of shelves pushed out into the room. Dee got her hand behind it and tugged the heavy door open enough for them to slip inside the secret passage. The air was damp, and the stone walls radiated a chill. Pitch-black.

"I can't see a thing," she whispered, her voice almost silent.

The familiar sound of the Imagination Box working echoed in the darkness, and then, about ten seconds later, the space lit up and Tim had a flashlight in his hand.

"Ta-da," he said as the tunnel appeared in front of them.

A handle at the far end glistened in the light. They headed down the long, spacious corridor, and Tim pushed the door open.

Inside, they were greeted by the sight of a huge, cluttered laboratory. The flashlight beam picked up the floating dust that explored the still air. The place looked expensive but neglected. Only one or two worktables were clear. The others were piled with old junk. One shelf had nothing but electrical equipment on it, dangling wires and circuit boards jutting out at all angles. Their eyes followed the light as Tim swept it round to the right-hand end of the room. Two large metal cylindrical chambers, the size of coffins, stood side by side, connected by thick wads of cables. Each had a small glass window in the center. They looked like something you'd find on a submarine.

"Look at this," Tim whispered.

"What is it?" Dee squinted.

They went closer. Tim felt cool air clinging to his clothes. "It's a teleporter," he announced, lighting up one of the cylinders.

"How can you be so sure?" Phil asked. "It is just two metal things. It could be absolutely anything. You must remember never to assume, Timothy."

"It says 'teleporter' on it," Tim replied.

The flashlight beam fell on the bottom of the control box between the two chambers. It did, in fact, say "teleporter" on the side, followed by lots of numbers.

"Oh yes. So it does," Phil admitted.

"Do you think this is Professor Whitelock's?" Dee whispered. "You said someone stole his teleporter? But this is his wife's house. . . . Why would she—"

A creak came from somewhere in the building. They all froze. Tim clicked the flashlight off and placed his hand on Dee's shoulder. All he could hear was their tightened breathing and his own thrumming pulse between his ears.

"Timothy," Phil finally whispered, his voice trembling. "I am experiencing the physiological symptoms of fear. It does not feel good."

The light came back on. "All right," Tim croaked over his heartbeat. "Maybe it is time to leave."

They turned, but at the opposite end of the lab was another huge chamber, the size of a separate room.

"Hang on," Tim whispered, walking briskly across the concrete.

He and Dee inspected the chamber for some time before he realized what the machine was.

"Do you know what *this* is?" Tim said, peering in through one of its windows. It was empty. "I think it's an Imagination Box."

"It's gigantic." Dee looked up. It reached the high ceiling.

"Yes," Tim said. "It's a lot like your grandfather's prototype, only much bigger. But the reader is . . ." Tim glanced around near the control box.

He followed the wires and found empty plugs on the end. Then on a workbench against the wall, he spotted the reader connected to a laptop.

"Look at this," Tim said, picking it up. It was heavy, covered in complex components, and surely very uncomfortable to wear. It reminded him of a weird fighter pilot's helmet. "Why is it plugged into the computer, though?"

He pressed a key on the laptop, and the screen lit up instantly, only having been asleep. On the desktop was a folder marked "Reading Tests." Tim double-clicked it.

A groan emanated from the building—maybe a pipe— and Tim hesitated.

"The sensation is intensifying," Phil added. "I think our departure should be prioritized."

"In a minute," Dee said, stepping forward and looking down at the screen. There was a subfolder marked "Eisenstone." She moved Tim's dawdling hands away and clicked it open herself. It was empty. Back in the main folder she selected "Stephen's Tests." There was one file, called "Thought Read 1."

"Stephen's tests?" Tim wondered.

The screen went blank. Then colors and code spread across it, shapes and words, letters, numbers, symbols, abstract blobs—it was random nonsense. Then a picture of a thin, black-haired woman began to emerge, first as juddering digital squares, and then as clear as day. Clarice Crowfield. It was like footage from an old film, jumping and cutting roughly. Sometimes it rewound, sometimes it broke up and disappeared under smudges and lines.

She appeared to be happy, smart, young, and glowing, like she had been in that painting. She twirled in the sunlight, smiled into a mirror, and played tea towel peekaboo with the "camera," looking directly back at Tim through the screen. But then the image morphed, color drained, and she was screaming about something—all from someone else's point of view.

"These are memories," Tim said. "The reader has taken them from Stephen's head. It's his perspective we are seeing, and it must translate thoughts into . . . this."

A jumpy cut produced another memory. Early morning, a kitchen window. Again they saw from a low, child's perspective, wandering up the hall. Small hands were carrying a tray of what looked like a freshly made breakfast—pancakes, fruit, a glass of orange juice, all spread out beautifully. Even a flower in a small vase. The scene went blurry and fuzzy, and then sharpened as young Stephen arrived in Clarice's bedroom. She woke, frowning.

Then some shouting. A flash to the breakfast on the floor, smashed glass and ruined food, back up to Clarice, who was shaking her head. Tim lip-read, "Rubbish—absolute rubbish."

Other memories played out—blurred colors and ripples, and then Clarice was shouting, pointing, throwing things. "It's your fault," they lip-read her whispering. "I had so much potential, stolen by you. Think of what I could have done." Stephen's childhood had clearly been no treat. It seemed his mother placed at his feet the blame for all her failings.

Then the images on the screen leapt forward once more. Clarice stood over Stephen as he filled out an application form with the Dawn Star logo on top. They saw the hotel as Stephen saw it. It was brighter, somehow nicer than the reality. It was obvious he liked it—the memory was happy, positive, unlike most of those that featured his mother. Tim saw himself, saw that Stephen had been spying—taking pictures, keeping watch. The footage flickered again, though. All the color faded, and Eisenstone appeared. Stephen's hands crumbled pills, white tablets, into a drink.

A few more frantic distortions gradually slowed down. The word "sorry" appeared again, scrolling and rolling around on the screen, sometimes on paper, sometimes just floating through the air like smoke in a breeze.

"My goodness," Phil said.

"It was all her. Clarice put him up to it. . . . Poor Stephen." Tim closed the laptop lid. "I can't watch that anymore."

"They are using the reader to *look* at thoughts," Dee said, astonished.

"If you think about it, that's what readers are doing. Maybe this is just displaying them, rather than creating them?"

"It is amazing," Phil added. "To extract memories. And the empty folder? Is that what they are doing with Professor Eisenstone?"

"Maybe," Tim replied, still disturbed by the visions of Stephen Crowfield's dark past. "Maybe these memories are just an experiment. Perhaps they want to read the professor's mind to find out how he made *his* Imagination Box work?"

"So if that means they *have* kidnapped him," Dee concluded, "then where is he?"

Back in the study, Tim gently closed the door to the secret passageway behind them. It felt like they'd been in there awhile. The early-morning sun was now coming through the slit between the long curtains. Stephen's recorded memories had showed that he'd drugged and, most likely, kidnapped Eisenstone, all under the instruction of his mother. They'd been using the reader from their huge Imagination Box to do what the device did best—read minds. Clarice was obviously carrying on with Whitelock's work but, Tim suspected, wasn't particularly successful.

Sneaking, Tim and Dee went back to the boards covered with photos and notes. This was enough. This was the evidence they needed.

"Right," Tim said, pulling the Imagination Box from his backpack. He thought hard of a digital camera, compact, efficient, and high resolution.

"What is *that*?" Dee whispered as the lid slid open to reveal his creation.

Tim grumbled to himself as he pulled a postcard from the contraption. It had a *photo* of a camera on the front.

"It is a lovely picture," Phil said.

"All right, everyone be quiet." Again, Tim tried. This time he crouched, gently rubbing the sides of his head, trying to remain calm, ignoring the fact that he was halfway through a break-in. He imagined the camera's intricate electronics, the screen, the lens, and all the bits he didn't consciously understand, and finally the box whirred and his digital camera was born.

"That's better." Tim started snapping away. He took a picture of each board and a couple of the study. He also took a shot of Clarice Crowfield's large portrait and the shrine to her past. After a minute or so he felt he had enough.

"Timothy," Phil whispered. "I propose a noble retreat now. We can take our findings to Inspector Kane."

"Not yet. There was a door under the stairs," Dee said. "Maybe that's a passage to the basement? We should check there first—what if they *are* keeping him here?"

"She's right."

The monkey let out a deliberately dramatic sigh. "Fine, but let us be quick and, above all, silent."

In one motion Tim picked up his backpack from the floor and swung it onto his back. As he did so, the bag connected with a mug that was on the corner of the desk. They had been so cautious, *so quiet,* up until this moment.

Helplessly all three of them saw the china cup fly through the air, twirling and reflecting the dim light of the study. There was nothing they could do but watch as it fell to the hard, stone floor. It smashed with a tremendous amount of noise, sending shards of china sliding and spinning across the floor.

"Oh, deary me," Phil said. "I suspect this shan't end well."

CHAPTER 17

Crowfield House seemed to thump awake with commotion above them. Tim and Dee ran toward the exit but heard feet already on the stairs.

Someone was coming.

Tim slammed his back against the bookshelf behind the study door. There was no room for Dee, who spun round once, twice, looking for a place to hide. She hit the ground and rolled under the desk, getting out of sight just as Clarice Crowfield stormed in holding a baseball bat. Her face was half-asleep, but her body was wide awake. Long black hair hung down, unusually neat for someone who had been asleep moments ago. Tim stood in the shadow of the door, watching her crouch and pick up a shard of the mug.

"I know you're still here," she yelled, still with her back to where Tim was hiding. He could see Dee's panic-stricken face pinned down on the other side of the room. The monkey had burrowed as deep as possible into Tim's shirt pocket, his tiny heart beating rapidly on Tim's chest.

Clarice looked up to the desk where the mug had once been and then stalked toward the window. Like a suspicious dog, she smelled the air. This woman was even worse in the flesh than in Stephen's memories. Seeing her made this whole break-in altogether more real. Too real, in fact. Tim guessed that the woman, crazed from head to toe, would have no problems using that bat. He hastily gestured for Dee to come out, but Dee looked at Clarice standing right there, facing away, and frantically shook her head. Then she waved Tim off, silently mouthing for *him* to run. To go and get help. Maybe she was right, maybe that was his only option.

When Clarice inspected the opening to the secret passage, Tim edged his way around the door, holding his breath until it began to hurt. He saw her thin hand squeeze the bat. Then he leaned round to look into the hall. The coast was clear. Staying low, he darted out through the front door, leaving it wide open in his haste. He knew that shutting the door would have made a noise, and Tim could already hear Clarice shouting for Stephen, and the sound of someone tearing down the stairs.

Tim ran as fast as his legs would carry him onto the driveway, where he skidded to the ground and hid behind Stephen's black car. Lying on his front, he perched on his elbows by a back wheel, Phil hanging his furry head out of Tim's pocket. From here Tim could see Clarice— still clutching the weapon—and Stephen coming out, searching.

"Dee's still in there," Phil whispered.

"Yeah, I know. We've got to go and get help." Tim would be returning in good time, with Inspector Kane as support. "As soon as they've gone back inside, we'll make a break for it."

Blinking through the morning sun, Stephen scanned the front drive, sweeping his gaze backward and forward across the huge expanse of land surrounding the building. Then he slowly began walking toward the car—toward Tim.

"Oh no," Tim said, looking around for somewhere to go. He crawled farther, reaching up to one of the back doors, hoping hard that it was unlocked.

"Got ya," Stephen shouted as he leapt round to the side of the vehicle, but there was no one there. Standing up straight, he sighed.

Tim had gotten into the car, just in time. On the backseat he lay as still as he could, only a meter away from Stephen, who was searching the bushes nearby. And then, on the floor of the car, Tim spotted a familiar green hat and a camera with a telescopic lens.

"Can you see anyone?" Clarice yelled. "Stephen!"

"No, Mother." His voice echoed. "I'm going to have a drive around the grounds, see if I can find anything."

No, no, no, Tim thought, burying his face in his hands.

The driver's door opened and Stephen climbed in. Curled up in a ball on the backseat, Tim tensed every muscle. If Stephen looked up at the mirror, or behind him, that would be it—game over. But instead Stephen patted his bathrobe pocket and then climbed back out. No keys, Tim thought.

Phil clambered up onto the top of the seat. "Timothy, we have got to think of something. We have got to figure something out. A solution better than a jetpack," the monkey said. He began literally jumping up and down in panic. "He's coming, Timothy. He's coming back!"

But Tim was already in the front seat, the Imagination Box open next to him.

"What are you doing?" Phil asked, his voice quivering. "Timothy? Have you ever driven before?"

"I have sat in a go-kart," Tim replied as he lowered the handbrake down and looked at the steering wheel in front of him. "Once." He pushed the key he'd just created into the ignition.

"So . . . no, then."

"I suppose not. Phil, come here. You have to direct me—I can't see over the dashboard."

"This seems to be a dangerous idea."

"Yes, it is, but unless you've got a better one . . ."

Tim reached up and adjusted the inside mirror. Stephen was almost upon them.

"Go!" Phil yelled as he leapt into the front.

The car rumbled to life, and Tim rammed the stick into drive, relieved that the car was an automatic. Stephen stopped just behind the car, seemingly bewildered that it had started. He looked at his own keys and frowned. The vehicle pulled away with spinning wheels, gravel and mud flinging up around him.

"Okay, Phil, which way?" Tim asked.

The monkey was clinging on to the dashboard, inches from the windshield. "Right," he said. "Turn right."

The car gently swayed *left,* its wheels getting caught on the grass. It jolted and bounced off the pavement, slowing dramatically.

"The other right!" Phil yelled.

Tim remembered the walk up to the house. He guessed the gate was perhaps three hundred meters away. After getting back onto the road and straightening the tires, he pushed the accelerator pedal and gently pulled the steering wheel round, feeling the speed increase. Faster and faster. He couldn't see anything at all—he had to trust the directions.

"More right," the monkey said. "Less right. Less right."

"So, left?" Tim screamed.

"No. Less right."

"'Less right' is left!"

"No, it isn't."

Two wheels were on the road, two were on the grass. Again the car had slowed, and Stephen grabbed the back door and managed to get it open. Tim looked round, swerving as he did so. Stephen stumbled and lost his grip. They swung up onto the grass, and then, without Phil's directions, Tim pulled it back toward the long driveway.

"Okay," Phil said. "Good. Now a tiny bit right, then a bit more, then a bit more."

"Your directions are confusing!" Tim shouted. He took his foot off the accelerator and knelt up on the seat to look out the windshield, seeing the curve of the drive all the way down to the large iron gate.

"Quick!" Phil yelled.

Tim sat back down and slammed his foot onto the pedal as Stephen threw his body at the back of the car, bouncing the suspension, but he slipped and went tumbling over and over on the road. The car weaved, picking up more and more speed as they approached the gate. Tim knew he'd have to hit it with quite some force to go through.

"Left a bit, left a bit," Phil said, pointing at their small target. He then began screaming. They sped closer and closer, the engine straining.

Tim, eyes shut, gripped the wheel more tightly, and braced himself.

They smashed through the gate, sending the cast iron scraping across the car's roof. Birds erupted from nearby foliage. Bricks and lumps of metal spun in the air as the car screeched onto the road, scattering debris everywhere.

"We did it," Phil yelled.

"Now where?"

"Keep going. It's pretty straight."

They drove for a while. Tim checked the mirror to see they weren't being followed. Behind them was the entrance, utterly destroyed, and farther back, Crowfield House, still proud on top of the hill. They approached a turnout, and Tim slowly pulled in, with careful directions. They toyed with the idea of driving all the way to the police station but, with adrenaline fading, decided against it.

"I can't believe it," Tim said. "We made it. We made it without crashing. Well, apart from the crash. No *accidental* crashes, though."

They were still rolling when Phil jumped down onto the seat.

"Counterfeiting money, burglary, car theft, trespassing . . . any other crimes you feel like doing today, Timothy?"

"Hey, I didn't steal anything from inside the house. Take back 'burglary.' "

"I think it counts; you still broke in."

"*We* broke in, Phil. Quite successfully too. And the getaway went well, I think."

"With my directions and your expertise, we are unstoppable. We should do rally racing," Phil said.

"I know! A very, very successful first drive. Well done, team."

"Hang on a second." Phil looked over his shoulder, then down at the seat. "We are still moving."

The front wheels hit the mud of the deep ditch at the edge of the road, and the hood disappeared down, thumping into the dirt.

Tim was flung forward and caught by his seat belt, and Phil landed on the cracked windshield. The Imagination Box bounced and ended up hanging by a strap off the top of the passenger seat. The car was stuck, almost vertically, in the base of the trench.

"Hand brake," Tim groaned. "Well . . . I'm sure he has insurance. We've probably done him a favor."

They quickly clambered out and ran into the woods as the warm sunrise burst through the trees. Long columns of light came between branches, making glitter of the morning dew. But there was no time to appreciate it—they had to head down the hill, into town, to the police station, to tell Inspector Kane what they'd found. And they had to be fast. Dee was still trapped inside the house, completely at the mercy of the Crowfields.

CHAPTER 18

Tim was out of breath when he arrived at the back of the police station. He'd jogged all the way there, down the hill, through Pine Common, and across Glassbridge. It took well over an hour, his pace slowed by exhaustion. Throughout the whole journey he'd been anticipating the look on Inspector Kane's face when Tim would show him these pictures, tell him about the memories they'd seen on the computer. You want hard evidence? Well, here it is.

On the way, Phil had suggested that Tim create a phone, which he had, but despite repeated attempts they hadn't been able to get a signal. Assuming he wasn't making things properly because of stress or tiredness, Tim had blamed himself for the failing. Then, to vent his frustration, he'd thrown the phone at a tree.

Reaching the police station, he swung his legs over a low metal barrier in the parking lot and crossed the pavement to an alleyway at the side of the building, leading to the front and the main entrance.

"Phil, inside. We're nearly there," Tim said, stepping over a small bag of rubbish. The monkey disappeared inside Tim's shirt pocket.

Just as they arrived on the street, Tim was surprised to hear Elisa's voice. He shot back into the alley and slammed himself against the bricks, then squatted down behind a large bin and peeked around it. She was crying. He heard Chris's voice, which was strange, because Chris was supposed to be away on business.

"But why isn't he taking it more seriously?" she said through tears. Chris hugged her tight. They were standing right in front of the station door. "I don't care what he says. I'm sure this has something to do with Eisenstone."

"It's fine. Like he was saying, kids usually turn up safe," Chris said. "You never ran away when you were young?"

"No, never. Where would they go?"

"Let's get home, all right? Tim might have already come back."

"Okay," she said, and sniffed.

"Besides, breakfast is in full swing, and those waitresses aren't going to shout at themselves. The hotel can't run without its backbone."

"I don't care about the hotel," she said.

They walked past the mouth of the alleyway, Chris with his arm round Elisa. Tim leaned back behind the bin, deep in the shadow, so they didn't see him.

"Timothy," Phil said.

"Shh!" He wrapped his hand over his pocket.

Phil struggled and mumbled as he tried to break free. "Mmmtimm, Tim." Tim released his grip. "Why are you hiding? Go and speak to Elisa, let her know you are okay."

"No."

"Why not? She was crying."

"She . . . she'll be fine. Look, we ran away, a huge breach of the rules. I'm going to be in *massive* trouble. Once I've delivered the camera and fixed all of this, then we'll face the music."

"Timothy, I feel you are being quite unreasonable. If you gave her more of a chance, you would see that she just wants what is best for you."

"Phil . . ." Tim sighed, lifting the monkey from his pocket and placing him on the bin's lid. They were eye to eye. "If she sees me now, she'll be furious. You don't know what she can be like. She'll—"

"If you explain it to her, she will be able to help—"

"I don't need help," Tim said, feeling an odd mix of emotions after Elisa's tears. He'd never seen her that upset. He'd been surprised to see sadness, not anger. "I've been by myself long enough now, and it's fine," he added with a shrug. "I don't need her. . . . I don't need anyone."

"Timothy," Phil said very deliberately. "If that is true . . . then . . . why did you create me?"

And, right there in that alleyway, Tim stopped and nodded, realizing that maybe, just maybe, he wasn't okay with being alone.

"That's a sound point, little monkey," he said. "A sound point."

Tim held his shirt pocket open, and Phil leapt back in.

"Let us sort this pickle out," Phil said, looking up. "Once and for all."

Inside Glassbridge Police Station, Tim walked right past the receptionist, who'd clearly only just arrived for work. "Um, excuse me," she said behind him, fussing with her handbag, but he just kept going. He banged Inspector Kane's office door open.

Thankfully, despite the early hour, the policeman was sitting at his desk, sipping coffee and flicking through the newspaper. The page was open to the travel supplement, and photos of exotic islands stretched across the page in vivid color. He lifted his head.

"Listen, I've got something to show you," Tim said.

"Um, good morning?" Kane closed the paper.

Tim pulled out his digital camera and threw it to Kane.

"Look at the pictures on there," Tim said. "Dee's at Crowfield House. Pretty sure Professor Eisenstone is too. You've got to help them."

Inspector Kane held the camera. He was being infuriatingly slow. "You look very tired, Tim. You getting enough sleep?"

"No, not really. Been up all night. Plus there's this sort of demon monster that crawls through the vents in the Dawn Star. Really scary thing. Please, look at those photos."

"Ah, I see. When I was young, it was under my bed. Every night I'd get my mother to check. I was convinced there was a clown or something down there. Your imagination can sometimes play tricks on you."

"Can't it just?"

Inspector Kane spent a few moments pressing buttons. He frowned as he flicked from one incriminating photo to another.

"These were taken in the study of Crowfield House," Tim explained. "Clarice Crowfield married Professor Eisenstone's former partner, Professor Bernard Whitelock, before he died. I believe Clarice and Stephen Crowfield, the Dawn Star's new chef, have kidnapped Eisenstone and are keeping him somewhere."

Clearing his throat, the policeman looked uncomfortable.

"And Dee is still there, still at Crowfield House," Tim added. "You've got to go there and fix this."

"I'll hold on to this for future reference. We'll see how it develops," Kane said. He opened his top drawer and placed the camera inside.

"What?" Tim said, bewildered. "You're not going to arrest them? Aren't you listening?"

"Tim, please lower your voice," the policeman whispered, glancing at the door. "I've just returned from Crowfield House myself. You could be in very big trouble."

Tim frowned. "Why were *you* there?"

"Why?" Kane coughed. "They called me about a break-in. I could arrest *you* for trespassing. Now, this is your last chance. Just *go home*."

"But the pictures. They've taken him. The longer we sit around here, doing nothing—"

"Tim, Tim, Tim. You've explained, very broadly, your theory. Well done, good work . . . but you haven't explored motive. *Why* would they want Eisenstone? Why kidnap him?"

Taking a long breath in, Tim tried to calm himself. He gave a lot of thought to his next words. Weighing up the pros and cons and having considered all the scenarios, he finally decided, for the first time in a while, to be open and honest. It was the only option left, the only way to make Kane take what he was saying seriously.

"Because of the importance of his work," Tim said.

"What does that mean? What do you know about his work?" Inspector Kane was leaning forward, speaking with another layer of worry in his voice.

"I know more than anyone else. I know more than his own daughter. I probably know more than Stephen and his scary mother, Clarice. And I certainly know more than *you*."

Screwing up his eyes, Kane cupped his face in his hand.

"Tim," he said, slowly shaking his head, "I told you to leave it, didn't I? I said it would be trouble if you carried on, but you didn't listen. I warned you."

"Inspector Kane, do *you* know what Eisenstone was working on?" Tim said, undoing the zipper on his bag.

"I know a fair bit about quantum physics. I read some of his book—"

Tim laughed. He looked across the desk. His eyes were drawn to a very posh pen.

"That's a lovely pen, isn't it?" Tim said.

There was a moment of silence. Kane seemed confused by the change of subject.

"Yes, yes, it is. My ex-wife gave it to me. She bought it in Chile."

"Did she?" Tim said. "Quite rare, is it?"

"I don't know if it's rare, but they don't make them in this country. Special wood. Plus, my name is engraved on the side. . . . Anniversary gift."

"Strikes me as quite a coincidence that I have one too," Tim said, reaching into his bag and pulling out a pen identical to Kane's. "Strange, that." He threw it onto the desk and sat back in silence.

The inspector saw that it was exactly the same as his own—same material, same tiny font spelling his name. He lifted his head. "Where . . . where did you get this?"

"I made it. I made it in something called an Imagination Box. *That* is what Eisenstone was working on. A machine that creates anything you can imagine from the ground up, atom by atom. Things like a sausage, a jetpack, a nightmare, and even a self-aware, miniature monkey who is perhaps more articulate than I am."

Tim then pulled out the device and put it on Kane's desk. The cube, sleek and silver, greeted Inspector Kane's eyes. The question mark on the side was facing him. The inspector admired the craftsmanship. Then, slowly, he shook his head again—this time in awe.

"Where did you get *that*?"

"You want to know where I got it? I made it. I made it in Eisenstone's machine. I made my *own* Imagination Box."

"That's impossible."

"Well, actually"—Tim pointed at the device on the desk—"no, it isn't. Listen, I think the people who have taken Eisenstone want to make their own version of this.

175

I saw a *huge* prototype in a secret lab in their house. You have to help me. It's not too late to save him."

Kane looked, for some reason, as though he had just been delivered some sad news. "Tim . . . I . . ."

"We've got to go to Crowfield House," Tim said.

"Yes," the policeman replied, standing, sighing, and looking down at his feet. "I think you're right."

Glassbridge police station's underground parking lot smelled of damp concrete and exhaust fumes. A pipe dripped nearby. Kane looked over his shoulder, as though to be sure no one was around, then opened the back door of his car. Tim eased his backpack off, about to climb in, but without saying a word, the policeman snatched the bag from him. Tim was more confused than worried at first.

"Get in," Kane said. "Now." When Tim hesitated, wondering why Kane seemed so firm, the inspector grabbed him by the arm. "I said, *get in.*"

"Wait," Tim said, realizing something was wrong. He tugged away, but before he could get completely free, the policeman picked Tim up and threw him over his shoulder. As Kane did so, Phil went flying out of Tim's top pocket and landed on the pavement. The monkey quickly scurried out of sight under the car, as Tim was bundled into the backseat.

A moment later, the wheels screeched and the car

pulled up the ramp onto the road. Tim listened to Kane's muffled voice as he made a phone call in the front seat. He was repeating what Tim had told him at the station. At the end of the conversation, Kane said, "Yes, you need to get rid of everything, and I want the rest of my payment today. The pressure . . . it's mounting. I want every penny. I need to be gone. Then we're done. All right, Clarice, see you in ten."

There it was, there was the answer to their question— this was why Kane had been so reluctant to investigate: he was working with the Crowfields. Tim silently cursed himself for being so *foolish*. For getting carried away, for not stopping to think. Feeling terribly alone, he grabbed his chest, holding the space where Phil should have been. The monkey was by himself now, in that parking lot, and Tim wished hard that Phil wouldn't stray any farther from home.

And so Inspector Kane did as Tim had asked and took him back to Crowfield House, but for all the wrong reasons.

CHAPTER 19

When they arrived, Kane took Tim by the shoulder and shoved him firmly through the front door into Crowfield House's hallway. It looked different in broad daylight, somehow grander. Tim felt hopeless, unarmed, without his Imagination Box. The corrupt policeman had hold of it the whole time.

Tim turned and tried to push past, but Kane was too big and heavy to move out of the way. Without speaking, the inspector pulled Tim by his collar and dragged him into the study. Tim stumbled inside. In front of him, by the desk, Stephen and Clarice Crowfield were waiting. The young chef averted his eyes, perhaps ashamed of what he'd done, while Clarice casually inspected her fingernails. Tim worried about Dee. Had she gotten out? Had she managed to escape like him? He felt a twist in his stomach, terrible guilt. He had left her so that he could get help . . . only to return with just the opposite.

"Ah, our little intruder," Clarice said with a clap.

The police officer silently held out Tim's Imagination Box, and Tim watched on in horror as it fell into Clarice's skinny hands. In turn she passed over a duffel bag, and then Kane, the one man Tim had thought could help him, looked down at the floor, sighed to himself, and left with his payment slung over his shoulder. Clarice pulled the contraption straight from the backpack and burst out laughing, a crazed cackle echoing around the high-ceilinged study.

"You?" she said. "You've made it work? All the secrets, all we need, wrapped up tightly in your tiny little skull." Clarice leaned down and grabbed Tim by the cheeks. "Would you like to show us how your atomic constructor works, Tim?"

"No, not really," he replied. "And it's called an Imagination Box."

"That's . . . that's actually a nice name," Clarice said. "That's much better. Stephen, why didn't *you* think of that?"

Her son stepped forward. "Why don't we dismantle the box to see if—"

"Stephen, you tapeworm's tapeworm." Clarice tensed her jaw, without turning. "When I want your input, I'll ask for it."

"Right," Tim said. "You guys are absolute fruitcakes. Crackers. That's obvious. But, come on, this is getting out of hand. You need to grow up. Where's Eisenstone?" Tim was testing the water. He was still unsure exactly what these guys were capable of. Perhaps he could talk his way out of here?

"Eisenstone?" Clarice frowned.

"Yes, I know you kidnapped him," Tim added. "Let us both go, and I'll show you how the Imagination Box works. I'll even teach you to use it. That's what you want, isn't it?"

Clarice clapped her hands and threw her head back. Her features looked distorted when she smiled. Behind, above the desk, her portrait seemed a different woman. Tim imagined she was once quite pretty, but now it was as though all the color were gone from her.

"I love this boy," she squealed, all teeth and gums. "Trying to buy his way out. How endearingly optimistic." She leaned down in front of him and ruffled his hat, oblivious to its being an integral part of his Imagination Box. "You, my young boy, are in no position to bargain with us."

"What do you want from me?" Tim asked, pulling away.

"If you actually have a working atomic—Imagination Box, then we'll need to take it apart for answers."

"Take it. It's yours," Tim said.

"Still trying, bless." She tilted her head. "You broke my favorite mug and my gate, and you crashed Stephen's car. I'm afraid it's just not an option for you to leave here intact. Loose ends, you understand."

Clarice clicked her fingers, and Stephen stepped forward and grabbed Tim's arm. Tim struggled and tried to tug away.

"I'm sorry," Stephen said.

"No, let go!" Tim yelled. "Get off. Get off!"

As Clarice approached, clutching a black bag, he kicked and twisted his body. She slammed it onto his head, plunging him into darkness. Then he felt himself being carried. He thrust and wiggled for some time until he realized it was no use. After a while, he was dropped onto the ground, and he heard a door slam behind him. It was bolted shut before he got the black bag off. Rattling the door handle proved useless.

Dark, dingy, and smelly—this place was a fitting home for a prisoner. After a while his eyes adjusted, and gradually he saw more and more. There was a mattress on the floor, and the door had a small window with three vertical bars, which looked out onto a hallway.

A figure sat, hunched over, in the corner.

"Hello?" Tim whispered.

"Tim? Tim! Is that you?" the professor said, standing and stepping forward, out of the shadows.

"Eisenstone?" Tim ran and hugged him tight.

"Yes, yes. I'm so very happy and so very . . . so very sad to see you. Indeed. Why on earth are you here?"

"It's a long story. But I've found you, I've finally found you. I knew something was wrong. I knew you wouldn't go without saying goodbye. You left your watch at the hotel. I went full detective."

The fact that he was now in as much trouble as the professor didn't dampen his burst of happiness. However, he quickly came back down to earth when he thought of Phil and Dee.

"Oh yes, yes, yes, the watch. Yes. Tim, yes I did. I've been in this terrible, terrible place the whole time. But why are you here, in this cell?"

"I'm sorry. I told Inspector Kane all about the Imagination Box. I thought if he knew, it would make him more likely to find you. I didn't realize he was part of the scheme. I mean it's just so . . . unprofessional. I've gone right off him after all this."

"Yes," Eisenstone said. "Indeed, quite the snake."

They both sat on the edge of the mattress, on the floor. Tim realized he had to come clean about what he'd done in the lab that day when the professor had left him alone.

"You made *what*?"

"I created my own Imagination Box," Tim explained. "Wished for more wishes."

Eisenstone was flabbergasted. "And . . . indeed . . . I mean, does it work?"

"Most of the time, yeah. Can be a bit inconsistent, but on the whole it's good. Plus, look, the reader is actually just a woolen hat." Tim passed him the black beanie.

"Astonishing."

After he'd put it back on his head, Tim explained everything he'd done since they'd parted ways.

"All by yourself? Quite amazing."

"I wasn't . . . I wasn't by myself. . . . Dee helped."

"What? Why?" Eisenstone had terror in his voice. "Where is she now?"

"Not sure. . . . Last time I saw her, she was hiding under the desk upstairs." Tim nervously scratched his scalp. "To be honest, I've made a bit of a mess out of all this. Not quite as clever as I thought I was."

"Oh," Eisenstone sighed, worn by fear. "I suspect if they'd caught her, she'd be in here with us. Let's take comfort in her absence. Indeed."

"Yes . . . I'm sure she's fine," Tim said, despite not being sure at all. "We saw their giant Imagination Box upstairs, their reader. . . . What are they planning?"

"Clarice . . . she . . . I think she wants to take credit for it. She's hell-bent on making it work. I shudder to think what she intends to create inside."

"And the teleporter? We saw that too. Is that White-lock's?"

"Yes, yes. I saw it only briefly, but I'm fairly certain that's the one he built."

"So, how come it's here? You said someone burned his lab and stole it. Was it her? His own wife? She killed him?"

"It . . . it seems so. I was never introduced to Clarice, but I heard through the grapevine that he'd met some-one. Perhaps this was her plan all along. Maybe that's why she married him. We'd grown distant, Whitelock and I. . . . He was a different man. There was an . . . an in-cident, and he was, shall we say, in a vulnerable state of mind. . . . But I still can't see how he could marry such a woman. But I suppose he was . . . in love."

Tim wanted to press the professor further about his old partner, about why they had drifted apart, about what had actually happened between them. It felt as though there were things Eisenstone was not sharing. But the subject seemed to upset the professor.

"So," Tim said, "they've been trying to read your mind, right? To find out how the box works? We saw an empty folder on their laptop in the lab."

"That's right, yes, indeed. I've managed to resist it so far, managed to take my thoughts elsewhere."

"Right. I know it's a big secret and everything. I understand that the technology can be misused, wrong hands, got to be safe, I get all that, but were you not tempted to just tell her?"

"No. Because then she'd come after *you*," the professor said. "Your mind—your imagination—that's where their answers lie."

Tim smiled at the thought of Eisenstone's protecting him. "Well, I'm here now. Is there some kind of deal we could come up with? A compromise?"

"Ah, no, no. Tim. No, sadly, that won't work. It is imperative, crucial, and essential that we escape. I really can't overstate that. Indeed, yes, yes. We *must* escape. You see, when they are finished with us, once they've made their Imagination Box work, they are going to put us in the teleporter."

"To go where?" Tim asked.

"Nowhere."

"Um?"

"Oh my, yes. Remember I explained how a teleporter works? We will in fact disappear from the first teleportation chamber, but they'll ensure we never arrive in the one next to it. Deconstructed but not reconstructed. Wiped, as it were, off the face of the earth."

"Hmm," Tim said. "Doesn't that seem a little . . . insane? Clarice is off the chart."

Eisenstone nodded.

"So, fine, escape it is. . . . How?" Tim said.

"Where's Phil?" the professor asked. "He's quite small, nimble. He could help."

Wishing once again for the monkey's safety, Tim explained that he'd fallen from his pocket in the parking lot.

"Ah, a shame indeed. Right, okay. They've got *your* Imagination Box. It's only a matter of time before they take it apart. Oh yes. We need a plan. Come on, Tim, get your thinking cap on."

"Okay, right. The door is locked; that's obvious. Wait, what . . . That's it." Tim stood up.

"Well . . . I . . . yes . . . ?"

"Get my thinking cap on."

"Well, indeed."

"I've got it on! I'm wearing my hat. The reader. I can use it from here. I can make something right now . . . something that can save us . . . something that can defeat them. . . . Hmmm." Tim thought quietly for a moment. "There. Done. Now . . . we wait."

About ten seconds later, there was an almighty roar from upstairs. "BEEEEES!" Stephen shouted, his voice thundering through the vast building. "Very angry bees!"

Tim had, in actual fact, created robo-bees—cybernetic insects programmed to attack everyone upstairs and then fly down to the basement and etch away at the door with their miniature drill-stingers. As he'd hoped, a few of the tiny silver things arrived. Their buzz sounded digital as they started to work on the concrete around the hinges, and, standing by the barred window, Tim could see a tidy pile of dust forming beneath them, on the other side of the door.

They were a good inch through when Clarice stomped down to the cell.

"Oh no, you don't," she said as she bashed them to death in the darkened hall. "Tim. That was pretty smart," she huffed through the bars, straightening her hair. "It was incredibly dangerous—I could have been stung. However, I managed to lock Stephen in the lab to deal with them. Anyway, I need that hat. I assume it is the reader. Yes? The reader for your box?"

"Nope," Tim said from the darkness. "Just a regular old hat."

Clarice tapped on the bars. "Come on, cough it up."

Tim turned to Eisenstone, who gave him a quick nod, so he removed the reader and passed it through a hatch at the bottom of the door. Clarice's fingers, five little twigs, waited and then snatched it.

"A mobile reader . . . very, very clever," she said, turning it over to look. "Thank you, Tim. Goodbye. For now."

Later, in the faint, gray light of their prison, Tim stood up and walked from one wall to the other, pressing against each. "There must be a way out, there must be."

The lock at the end of the corridor clanked open and footsteps came toward the cell.

"That's Stephen," Eisenstone quickly whispered. "This is our only chance. Indeed, I think if we catch him in the right mood, he might let his guard down."

Tim nodded. The professor held his index finger up to his lips. Stephen's profile could be made out through the bars.

"Food," he said.

The hatch in the door opened, and two bowls of lukewarm porridge were pushed in.

"Nice trick, kid," Stephen said.

"Oh, the bees? I am sorry. I didn't want you to get stung."

"Well, I did. Lots."

"Look, listen," Tim said. "What are you doing? You're going to be in just as much trouble as your mother. I know it's not your fault, but the police won't know that. You can't take the blame for what she does. You've got to let us out of here."

"No. I can't. I can't. Mother . . . she will . . ."

"Indeed, yes, we'll make it look like we escaped by ourselves," Eisenstone added.

Stephen fidgeted and checked up the corridor. "Right, okay," he whispered. "I'll come back—"

"STEPHEN!" a voice bellowed from upstairs.

"I'm sorry, I'm sorry, I have to go. I'm sorry." He disappeared up the hall, the door at the end clunked, and with its lingering echo, he was gone.

Suddenly one of the bowls of porridge exploded, splattering sloppy oats onto the floor and up the wall. Frantically gasping for air, Phil tried to get the thick food off his face as he clambered out.

"Ah!" he wheezed, clutching his tiny throat. "Ah, air! Precious, beautiful oxygen."

"You're here," Tim said. "You little hero."

"I hid . . . hid in the . . . porridge. . . . I nearly . . . I almost drowned . . . in porridge," Phil said, and groaned. "That is *not* how I wish to die."

"You came for me," Tim said.

"Really, it is no problem." Phil's voice was croaky. "My pleasure."

"How did you get here?"

"Mostly . . . rooftops, telephone wires. I am quite the climber, it seems. Then I sneaked into the house through a . . . a cracked window frame."

"You were upstairs? Did you see Dee?"

"I am afraid to admit I did not. Let us hope that she managed to get away safe and sound."

"Yes, yes, yes. Good. This is good," Eisenstone said, thinking. "Indeed, yes. This might just be our ticket out of here. If you can sneak up there, oh yes, Phil, we may very well be able to . . . escape."

The monkey, being small enough, planned to make his

way upstairs, where he'd steal the keys to the cell and bring them down. Their last hope, their last chance, went through the bars with the odd oat still clinging to his fur.

"Good luck, Phil," Tim said.

"See you soon, chaps."

However, not two minutes after the monkey left, Clarice and Stephen arrived. She had a wheelchair, and he was holding a length of rope.

"We're ready," she said, opening the cell.

CHAPTER 20

Stephen had handcuffed Eisenstone to the old-fashioned wheelchair, and Clarice tugged Tim along by his shirt collar. They approached the bookshelf in the corner of the study, the secret entrance to the lab. Across the room, Tim spotted Phil, poised on the desk, leaning from behind the antique lamp. True to his word, he held a set of keys in his tiny paws. Tim shrugged helplessly as they went through the passage behind the books, stepping over countless dead metal bees strewn across the floor.

Once inside the cold, gloomy lab, Tim's eyes locked onto his Imagination Box. It was intact on one of the worktables, but his reader hat had been changed. They'd put wires in it, and it was now attached to *their* reader.

"Tim, come here," Clarice said, pulling him closer.

"What are you doing?" he asked, glancing up at their huge steel machine.

"Not that it's any of your business, but having inspected your Imagination Box, it seems hardware really is not our problem," Clarice said, fiddling with an exposed circuit board. "In fact, our device is perfect. The issue is software. The problem is our minds. Our imaginations. That's why Professor Eisenstone couldn't make his work either. Not until *you* showed up. Perhaps it's because you're a child. Perhaps you're a genius. Who knows?"

Tim couldn't help but feel a little bit proud again—he liked being the only one able to make the invention work, even if he didn't fully understand why. "But what have you done with my reader?" he asked.

"We've wired it up to ours. Two readers, one atomic constructor—Imagination Box. Now the only thing left to do is to use your head to make it work." Clarice leaned forward. "Then I'll know for sure if mine is built correctly."

Clarice stepped back and began untangling the cables connecting the readers.

"Wait," Tim said. "So you're going to get me to imagine things for you?"

"No," she sighed, as though he were being stupid. "I'm

going to imagine something. Then my reader is going to send that thought into your brain, then into my box. We're using you as a signal transmitter, nothing more."

"Well, no. I refuse," he said with a shrug.

"You know what, Tim?" she whispered. "I was sort of hoping you'd say that. Stephen!" she yelled.

Her son flicked a switch, and the other end of the large laboratory lit up, a bright white beam throwing shadows across the floor. Tim saw the teleporter, the two tall chambers. In the left-hand one was a person—she was frowning behind the glass.

"Dee," Eisenstone shouted. "No!"

"Now," Clarice said, picking up a small control panel. "I press this button, and it's bye-bye. Poof. Gone. So why not just do exactly as I say, yeah?"

"Why?" Tim said, looking over to Dee, who silently tutted, rolling her eyes. "Why are you doing this?"

"Why!" Clarice narrowed her eyes, as though she were insulted by the question. "Do you know who I am?"

Tim shook his head. "Haven't a clue."

"*Exactly,*" she said. "I was going to be the prime minister one day. That's what they said. I was on my way up. Can you imagine what it feels like to have everyone know your name, to be voted in by the people, to represent all the residents of Glassbridge, your neighbors, your friends, your family—only to then disappear, to become a *nobody*?" She turned to Stephen. "To have your career cruelly curtailed by a screaming, whining little baby?"

"So you're going to pretend *you* invented the Imagination Box?"

"Pretend?" She laughed. "Look at what I've achieved. This is *real*. My name will go down in history."

"Okay . . . I think I get it. Your methods are a little iffy, morally," Tim said. "But I get it."

"Oh, young man, judge me by my *results*."

"And, plus, I don't know *that* much about politics," he said, lifting an eyebrow. "But I was under the impression there were easier ways of gaining some popularity."

"You'd think so, wouldn't you?" she said. "You'd think your dear husband wouldn't be completely helpless, useless, unable to make *anything* work."

"Bernard Whitelock," Eisenstone said, his head hanging, tears brewing, utterly defeated. "You married my best friend, and then you killed him. All for what? For this? To get his technology, to exploit him for his inventions?"

"Oh, but you've got it so, so wrong. He wasn't your friend, remember, not after what you did. . . . And, besides, I didn't kill him—just the opposite. I gave him everything he needed. . . . Isn't that right, Bernie?"

Eisenstone's gaze slowly lifted as a figure stepped from the side of their huge Imagination Box. Tim recognized the old man from the photo he'd seen—hunched, his eyes flashing in the darkness.

"Bernard . . . But . . . you're . . ." The professor's voice was shuddering, as though he were looking at a ghost.

Perhaps they were, Tim thought, as Professor White-lock limped toward them, alive in the shadows.

CHAPTER 21

"But . . . but . . . you're dead," Eisenstone said, his eyes darting around, searching for answers.

"Well, he's not, is he?" Clarice mocked. "Are you not paying attention?"

"The lab . . . it was burned down." The professor squinted at his old friend. "You . . ."

Silently Tim waited for further explanation. He was just as confused.

"Smoke and mirrors," Clarice said. "It was my idea, wasn't it, Bernie? I thought the best way to finance the research was to cash in his life insurance. It'd mean he couldn't leave the house—he'd have to work here, all day every day. Little did I know that Bernie was *hopeless* . . . We tried and we tried, but still we couldn't make our Imagination Box work."

"So you resorted to dirty tactics indeed." Eisenstone glanced at his trapped granddaughter.

"Well, nice guys finish last," Clarice added. "We tried softly, softly. Stephen stole your briefcase, even broke into your house once again to look for more notes. But when we heard you were leaving the country, there was only one thing for it. Kidnapping you was just a means to an end—don't take it too personally. Mind you, after what *you* did to him, wiping you off the face of the earth seems a reasonable punishment."

Professor Whitelock was fiddling with their reader— connected by countless cables to Tim's—yet it was obvious from his body language that he didn't like Clarice's words. Tim wondered what she meant. That was the second time she'd accused Eisenstone of doing something to his former partner.

Dee's muffled banging caught Tim's attention.

"I . . . I don't understand," Tim said, looking down the long room at the metal chambers, all bright under the spotlights. "Why the Imagination Box? I mean, if you can make a teleporter work—"

"It doesn't work," Whitelock snapped over his shoulder, through clenched teeth. "It never makes the subject reappear. It can break things apart, but it can't put them back together again. It's *never* worked."

"Well," Clarice said. "It certainly fulfills *my* needs." She wiggled the controls with a maniac's smile.

"Why is it so easy to destroy, and yet so difficult to create?" Whitelock whispered to himself.

Clarice twirled in the middle of the lab, surrounded by her victims. "Isn't it just wonderful what we have achieved together?" she said, glancing around. "A device up here"—she pointed at their Imagination Box—"meant to bring things into the world, and at the other end of the spectrum"—she swung herself round to face their teleporter—"a device to remove them from it."

Tim then spotted something small on the tile floor, peering from under one of the worktables. It was Phil. He lifted a tiny finger to his lips. Looking quickly away, Tim hoped no one else would notice Phil.

Whitelock thumbed a switch on the fixed panel next to their Imagination Box, and there was a loud, deep thud, followed by the familiar electric whoosh, like an old vacuum cleaner powering down. A few bulbs on top of the device flickered, glowing through the mass of electronics near the high ceiling.

"It's on," he said.

The tall machine dwarfed Tim. It was about the size of his bedroom and had windows, with thick rusted bolts around the edge and a large door at the front. Clarice stepped toward the contraption. She took a moment to peer inside, placing her hand on the glass. The excitement was all over her face. Not for the first time, Tim felt rhythmic surges of anxiety. The only feasible hope left was Phil. For now, Tim would just have to play along.

"Perhaps," she said, crouching to pick up their hefty reader, "it'd be best if Bernie tested it first." She passed the reader to Whitelock.

Clarice then pushed Tim's hat onto his head, and fiddled with a plug by his ear. Whitelock approached, now wearing their reader. Face to face they stood, connected to one another by lengths of different-colored wire that hung between them like they were pylons. Tim's reader was, in turn, linked up to their Imagination Box.

"Remember," Clarice added. "Bernie will imagine something, it'll go through your noggin, and then to the machine, so make sure you relax."

Tim shuddered from a slight tingling on his scalp, like the prickle of static electricity, as they began transmitting via his mind. Gradually, thoughts and images infected his brain; he could observe what Whitelock was thinking. He could sense his memories, see his past, and feel his emotions.

Sickened, Tim clutched his hat and began pulling it off. Clarice, standing behind, slapped her hands on top to hold it in place. The experience was so overwhelming, he could no longer see the room. Tim's entire consciousness was being hijacked. Thunder drummed in his head, followed by what sounded like a harsh, rising wind.

When he opened his eyes, there was absolute silence and he was in a different place. He could see notes, paperwork, and an old computer. There was daylight coming from a window. He looked down at his hands—he was an adult. Although conscious, he couldn't control his movements. He was merely an observer.

A noise caught his attention. He turned to see Eisenstone. But he looked younger, with brown hair and fewer wrinkles. They were in a different lab. It was a little like a hospital, with white surfaces and expensive equipment.

"Let's just do it," Tim said, but his voice was different. He was Whitelock. He was reliving a memory and could sense that this was years in the past.

Nearby was what looked like a dentist's chair. Through Whitelock's eyes Tim could see a reader. But it was different, it was giant—like a dome hair dryer—and it had its own stand and its own control box larger than the main part of the reader itself. There were warning stickers up the side, one sporting what Tim recognized as the symbol for radioactivity.

Whitelock sat down in the chair, looking up at the technology above his head. There was a loud electrical buzz, like the hiss of television static. He was excited—it was actually going to work. He was sure.

"You don't have to do this," Eisenstone said as he attached sticky pads to Whitelock's temples. "I want this to happen as much as you . . . but . . ."

"George, full power," Whitelock replied, looking him straight in the eye. "Let's just get it done. Let's make history."

"Indeed," Eisenstone said, now smiling. He checked his silver pocket watch.

Then Tim noticed the letters *TDACD* printed on the side of what looked like a very early prototype of the Imagination Box. Although he didn't know why, he was acutely aware that what they were doing was dangerous.

Eisenstone placed his finger on a large red button housed on a control box near the arm of the chair. As he counted down from ten, Whitelock closed his eyes.

". . . three . . . two . . . one."

Click.

There was that roaring wind again. Agony tore through him, every vein swelled, bone seemed to bend. Tim could feel every moment of it. There was screaming, deep, guttural. It sounded distant; then he realized it was coming out of his mouth.

A flash of hands, twisted in spasm.

Time stuttered and leapt forward. Lying on the floor, he could see the ceiling, blurry and spinning. The room was red with a rotating light above, whipping round and round. An alarm.

"Are you all right?" a voice asked, muffled, like an overheard phone conversation. He turned to see Eisenstone crouched next to him looking terrified. "Can you hear me? Are you all right?"

All at once, Tim knew what they'd done. He could sense that this day, this memory he was seeing, was the last time Professor Eisenstone and Professor Whitelock had worked together. Something went wrong, terribly wrong, with the experiment. The reader had been too powerful, and it had somehow damaged Whitelock's brain.

It had changed him.

The two professors, partners, had then gone their separate ways. Tim felt the ache of a lost friendship. Whitelock spent years alone, obsessively working on his teleporter and on a new Imagination Box. Speaking to no one, he kept himself to himself. He labored day and night, but couldn't make either machine work.

Tim now realized why Eisenstone had looked saddened, even ashamed, whenever the topic of his former partner arose. All these years he had blamed himself for what had happened—for the failed experiment. But Whitelock had insisted on being the guinea pig; he'd known the dangers.

The memories continued to flow into Tim. He now saw Clarice before she married Whitelock. She whispered into his ear. "Professor Eisenstone used you, he *used* you. He didn't care about the risks."

"But," Tim said, in Whitelock's voice, "I insisted. It was my choice."

"No," she went on. "He only cared about himself. We can get back at him *together*. We can be the first to make the atomic constructor work. We'll win. We'll beat him."

Clarice was nice to Whitelock at first. She helped him, loved him. Then she convinced him to fake his own death—she said it was the only way he'd be able to finance his work. He agreed. He did everything she told him to.

Tim relived a rushed wedding, a hatched plan—fire engulfed Whitelock's past, sending shadows jutting across his future. They moved his Imagination Box and his teleporter into Crowfield House, which became his home, his place of work, and then, eventually, his prison.

"Tell him I'm sorry," a faint voice said. Tim realized this was aimed at him. Whitelock was sharing his thoughts. "Tell him it isn't his fault—what happened that day, in the lab. He shouldn't blame himself. He doesn't need to feel guilty. It's not his fault. It's not his fault. It's not—"

"—working," another voice interrupted. "It's not working. You're not trying hard enough. Give it here."

Like a jolt from a nightmare, Tim was yanked back to

the real world. His vision refocused, like looking through water at first and then bursting above the surface and seeing clearly. It had seemed like a dream. It felt as though hours had passed, but they'd been wearing the readers for less than a minute.

Clarice had tugged the device from her husband's head. Tim and Whitelock stared in silence at one another. Initially Tim had thought what he'd seen was merely the jumbled contents of an old man's mind. But somehow he felt these memories had been recalled deliberately—as though Whitelock wanted someone else to see the truth.

"Let me have a go," Clarice said. "It seems safe enough."

Across the lab, Tim saw that Phil had scurried up to the teleporter and was tugging at the handle. He decided that the moment the monkey got it open, the very second Dee was out, he was going to make a break for Eisenstone's chair, and then for the door. They might all be able to escape this madness.

CHAPTER 22

Clarice Crowfield smiled—all her features distorted—as she lowered the large metal reader onto her head. Her long black hair was flattened, hiding much of her face. She looked truly mad.

"Right," she said, leaning close, eyes wide. "Let's try this properly, shall we? You ready, Tim? *Let's create something.*"

At the other end of the laboratory, Phil was still silently battling with the teleporter door. Tim knew that if he refused, Clarice could still obliterate Dee with the flick of a switch. Perhaps, he decided, helping her make something could buy them some time. It could open the window for an escape.

"Fine," Tim said. "Let's do it."

Stephen, Whitelock, and Eisenstone all looked on.

The two readers, connected to one another, began whirring. Although Tim *really* didn't want to see inside *her* mind, he decided to submit and allowed it to happen. Steadily, once again, thoughts that weren't his own traveled down the wires and infected his brain.

The contents of her psyche arrived all at once, in a big, timeless batch. The lab disappeared, his eyes rolled back. He felt darkness, loneliness, failure, anger. And then he saw fire—thick, swirling flames bellowing out of a building.

Finally, through the frantic flashes of insanity, something began to form—a shiny gold ingot, rotating slowly on a pedestal. This is what Clarice was imagining, he reasoned. Everything else he had seen had just slipped through the net.

The gold bar was clear—Tim could see it vividly. Just as he did with his Imagination Box, he envisaged all the finer details. But the image flickered, fizzed, as though a conflicting signal had arrived. Clarice simply couldn't focus, couldn't filter out the pollution. And then Tim felt something terrible, something uglier than he could ever have imagined.

From the abyss of her mind arose a low, haunting sound. Breathing. Something was there, something hidden in the emptiness. Her demon, waiting in the void. Distant gurgling, getting closer, louder until it became clear, until the madness, the hatred, was right there, right in front of him.

Tim could feel it, he could hear it, he could *see* it. Something that should never, ever exist in the real world. Then he became aware that the thought was traveling from his brain, down the cable, to the vast Imagination Box in front of him.

He yanked his reader off—the real world flooded in around him—and slammed it onto the floor. It was too late. The damage had been done. He took steps back, almost falling as he retreated. Eisenstone looked confused by Tim's fear.

Tim shook his head, tears in his eyes.

The machine drummed into life, like an orchestra hitting its climax. It flurried with all sorts of noises as mad flashes of light—blue, green, yellow, red, red, *red*—shot into the room. Tim looked up at Clarice, who was watching in awe. The dance of her eyes was like the composer's hand—up and down, left and right—commanding the sounds. Whitelock and Stephen too stared on. Even Eisenstone was amazed to see it working, despite his concern.

The contraption strained hard, steam shot from the vents, wires glowed, as the machine constructed *something* from Clarice's mind. Eisenstone gradually started edging his wheelchair backward with his feet, copying Tim's retreat.

"What's . . . in there?" Stephen asked.

A brutal thud echoed around the lab. Then another. Dust and brick crumbs fell from the ceiling. Lightbulbs wobbled, sending shadows dancing. Everyone took a step back. Then another thump, the loudest yet. Circuits buzzed, and then the lab fell back into silence.

An explosion ripped the front of the chamber open as a monster smashed out with ease. Sparks, shrapnel, and a cloud of smoke hailed its arrival. It broke its way free, growling over the twisted metal of the Imagination Box.

This was the embodiment of madness, of hate, of the darkness within Clarice. The creature stood like a gorilla, only it was huge, larger than an elephant—its back pressed on the high ceiling. Its flesh was red, covered in open sores. Half its body was bold and imposing; the other half looked lame and unfinished. And its face—there was no animal on earth that it resembled. It was simply a monster. No visible eyes, just hollow cavities. Clear, sloppy drool dangled from its mouth. Razor-sharp teeth poked out, some breaking through the skin. Its head bobbed up and down as it heaved deep breaths, vapor shooting with each exhalation. Like a lion, its throat rumbled as it took in its new environment.

No one in the room knew what to do. No one knew what to expect. For the first time Tim tore his gaze away to see Eisenstone, who looked as though he were about to faint. Clarice too looked terrified—perhaps also wondering where her gold was.

The demon bellowed its war cry and leaned in, inches from her face, sending her hair swirling. It then heaved its body up into the air and slammed a fist down toward Clarice, who leapt backward as the floor spewed up from the impact.

"Oh my word," Phil said from Dee's shoulder, now by Tim's side.

She grabbed his arm. He flinched. "Tim," Dee said, "I think we should leave now."

The monkey had gotten her out, and, it seemed, just in the nick of time.

Tim nodded. "That's a good idea."

As the monster swung its heavy arm to the left, smashing a gaping hole in the wall, everyone burst into action. Eisenstone pushed himself back, slowly tilted in his chair, and then fell to the floor, still tied up. Grunting with every movement, the monster thundered toward Clarice, Whitelock, and Stephen, who quickly turned and ran their separate ways. Tim ducked toward the table behind the creature and grabbed a set of keys, then his Imagination Box and his reader. With his hands full, he returned to the professor. Dee was already on him, tugging and pulling, trying to get him back onto his wheels.

Tim fumbled with the keys as they all watched the

monster lurch for Stephen, who leapt over one of the lab tables and crouched behind. The beast's arm pushed into the wall above him, crumbling bricks as though they were sand.

Its attention then turned to Clarice. She picked up a stool and threw it. The wood shattered against its face. It didn't even react—rather, it advanced, destroying everything in its path.

She fell into one of the teleporter's chambers, the one Dee had left open, and sealed the door. Just as the monster lifted itself, about to destroy her, another stool bounced off its side.

Stephen looked as though he regretted throwing it, as the demon's head snapped round to him. It stomped sideways now, annihilating the table Stephen was hidden behind in two strikes of its heavy claws. Splinters and rubble stood in a dusty pile where Stephen had been. A pipe had broken, and water squirted out into the lab, splashing onto the animal's shoulder.

As Dee grabbed the keys from Tim and finally got Eisenstone's cuffs off, Tim watched Stephen crawling, scrabbling away to the other side of the room, where Whitelock was hiding.

Now the creature slowly turned again, to face Eisenstone, Dee, and Tim.

They frantically untied the leg ropes as the monster

plowed forward. It picked up a hefty lab table and flung it spinning through the air as the professor stood, free from his restraints. All three of them dived in different directions—and then rolled over to see the wheelchair gone, smashed to pieces against the wall.

Led now by Eisenstone, Tim and Dee ran toward the door, ducking another of the creature's swipes. This separated them slightly, and before Tim could catch up, he was struck and knocked from his feet. He skidded and bounced like a rag doll across the floor, and then thumped to a stop against the warped metal of the huge, broken Imagination Box. Then, without a beat, a supporting beam from above fell in front of him, followed by a mountain of bricks so high that he could no longer see the others.

His legs were trapped. As he tried to free them, he heard a curious, loud *conk* and felt a sharp ache on the top of his skull—a chunky piece of concrete landed by his side. It must have hit him, he thought, oddly relaxed. There was a faint taste of blood in his mouth and a hiss in his ears as his vision tunneled and then faded smoothly to black.

CHAPTER 23

The lab was calm. Things had started to settle; everything was becoming still. Tim blinked awake and touched a tender lump on his head. Still dazed, he watched Stephen crawl out from his hiding place. Everything was a blur. It all played out like a fever dream.

There was a distant banging, but Tim was still too dizzy to process it.

The destruction was extreme. The Imagination Box was in pieces, and piles of rubble sat on the floor beneath tall holes in the walls. Sunlight beamed in. It was a surreal thing to see. The laboratory seemed like a ruin from an ancient civilization—completely transformed in the short attack.

Tim watched Whitelock limp out of one of the new openings, off into the garden. He didn't look back.

The thumping continued, and Tim heard a faint voice.

To his right, at the other end of the lab, he saw Clarice locked inside the teleporter. She was hitting her fists on the inside of the window, yelling at the top of her voice. It sounded as though she were underwater.

Stephen looked through the bright light, which seemed suspended, almost solid, in the cloudy air.

"Let me out!" Clarice shouted, her yell softened inside the teleportation chamber. "Open this up, Stephen. Open it!"

He strolled toward his mother and gently grabbed the handle.

"Quickly," she said.

But with a deliberate tug, he snapped it off, locking her inside.

"Stephen? Stephen. Open this up now. You ungrateful little tick. You will open it." She pushed her hands against the glass, exposing her teeth. "I know you will."

Casually, purposefully, Stephen picked up the controls. He placed his thumb on the button.

"Stephen Crowfield!" she screamed. "You are a disgraceful, ghastly, repugnant lump of—"

He flicked the switch. Light flashed from the teleporter. Clarice fizzled and dissolved in an instant. Teleported to nowhere. Deconstructed but not reconstructed. Every atom, every particle that made her was now separated.

Clarice Crowfield was gone.

Stephen showed no remorse. Rather, his shoulders fell backward and his chin tilted up. Smiling, he turned and clambered out through the wall. He landed on the lawn, and escaped toward the trees at the back of the house.

Now alone, Tim wondered whether Stephen had been waiting his whole life for such an opportunity. Would he have done it if he'd known he was being watched? There was no way to be sure.

After Tim had cleared the debris from his legs, he scrambled to his feet and made it outside. When there was no sign of Eisenstone, Dee, or Phil, he went back in through the front door, and found them in the study.

"Tim!" Dee yelled. "You made it out. It's in there, in the passage to the lab."

Phil dived from her shoulder and slid straight down into Tim's shirt pocket. Tim quickly explained what he'd seen, but there was no time to discuss it. The secret bookcase was shut, and Eisenstone had tipped a tall, wooden clock onto its side and rammed it against the door.

"We need to keep it contained," the professor said over his shoulder. "Indeed, you two grab the desk—we need to trap it."

"What's going on?" a voice asked. They all whipped around to see Inspector Kane.

Eisenstone grabbed Tim's arm and shuffled him round behind himself, then did the same with his granddaughter.

"Yes, yes, what do you want?" he asked.

Kane held his hands up. "No, I'm . . . I'm sorry. I changed my mind. I don't want the money. It was wrong. I came back to rescue you."

The professor squinted, unsure whether to trust him or not.

"We don't need your help," Tim said.

"Yeah, jog on, Kane. You're not our friend," Dee added.

"Look, it doesn't matter now. Listen, listen, listen, we've got to get out of here," Eisenstone said. "There's a . . . It's a . . . a monster, indeed, yes, in there. We've got to go."

"A monster?" Kane laughed. "Sorry?"

He curiously approached the secret entrance.

"No, no, no. Really, stay back. Seriously," Eisenstone said.

The case vibrated; books rattled off the shelves. Below, the floor rumbled, and above, the chandelier clinked and wobbled. Kane took a few steps back.

Before he could say another word, the bookshelves exploded into a thousand pieces. The beast appeared. Eisenstone, Tim, and Dee went for the door as fast as they could. Looking back, Tim saw Kane holding his ground.

"Stop, police!" he shouted.

With a husky grunt, the monster tilted its head, as though contemplating the order. But then it snatched

215

Kane by the legs, swung him round, and threw him the full length of the room. He crashed straight through the window, disappearing from sight.

"Oh deary me," Phil whispered.

Behind them the creature began taking the study to pieces, like a toddler flinging toys in a tantrum. It made short work of the broad antique desk, rolling it over, sliding it across the floor, and then catapulting it over its shoulder. It ran its claws across the wooden shelves, turning them to wreckage with ease.

Everything it could see, it destroyed.

Tim, Eisenstone, and Dee all made it through the front door and outside. They stopped on the drive and turned back to the building as a desperate roar made birds flee from nearby trees.

"What now?" Tim said, catching his breath.

"Right, indeed, it mustn't get out," Eisenstone replied. "So long as it stays in there, we should be quite fine."

The side of the house gave way. The monster burst through and thudded onto the grass—a torrent of dusty debris and glass followed it.

Clarice's prized portrait landed on the ground amid it all. Her proudest moment, beautifully immortalized in the painting. The eyes looked toward the sky, at the mercy of the surrounding destruction. A moment later, the monster's heavy foot slammed down on top of the picture and twisted purposefully into the mud, crushing it like a finished cigarette.

The beast turned around and lumbered toward them.

"Back into the house!" Eisenstone yelled. He was right; there was no way they could outrun it on flat ground.

They made it inside, grabbing the door as the creature's face smashed against the wood on the other side. The professor used his back and tried to push the door closed. Dee and Tim too put their weight into it. Snarling breath blasted through the gap, and after a struggle the dead bolt clacked shut.

It sounded as though the beast had retreated.

"It's getting a run-up!" Dee shouted. They all sprinted toward the kitchen. Close behind, the monster broke in, destroying the doorway, the stairwell, and everything it passed through.

They only just made it to the back door in time, and charged outside once more. The monster came into the kitchen, twirling and obliterating. The building was collapsing behind it. Tons and tons of rubble fell, pinning the creature's lower half. It writhed and cried, flinging bricks, pots, and pans with every struggle. Its mouth stretched out and tore through the stove. The pipe split. Gas spewed out, filling the kitchen, making the air wobble like transparent jelly.

The story above had almost entirely collapsed, turning

the ground floor into a kind of pit. Walls stood with a hollow space in the middle, where the creature had trapped itself—upstairs furniture sliding, falling, smashing.

Crowfield House was in ruins.

On the grass at the back, Tim had an idea. He neatened his hat and closed his eyes. A few moments later, he opened his Imagination Box on the lawn, to reveal a small orange distress flare. Someone would need to light it and throw it into the gas.

Without saying a word, Phil clambered out of his pocket. He took it under his arm and headed back toward the building. Everyone else moved farther away.

They watched the monkey scurry up the twisted trellis and climb over the split walls to the tilting roof. From there he could see through all the floors, down to the kitchen. The demon was still struggling wildly, but with every movement Crowfield House tightened its grip.

Phil held the flare upright; it was twice as big as him. With both of his hands he tugged the tag to light it, teetering on a floorboard from the loft that jutted out at a strange angle. Below, the creature threw concrete off its back and stumbled into an open space, shouldering against the wall, stirring the gas. The monster was almost entirely free when Phil finally fired up the flare, which fizzed and sparkled hot, painting him red. From the ground Tim watched the bright glow appear at the corner of the house.

One final, defiant roar.

"Toodles," Phil said as he dropped it.

As it fell, he leapt outward, toward the grass. Tim watched the flare and the monkey descend in different directions, almost in a perfect reflection of each other. Before Phil hit the ground, the stick made its way into the heart of the gas leak. It clattered off a shard of tile and landed.

Fire, light, and heat burst out, all struggling to escape the quickest. The explosion was immense. The shock wave hit them like the front of a hurricane. They shielded their faces as the mushroom cloud rose, curving in on itself.

Tim's eyes scanned the grass, desperate to see Phil. Building pieces rained down, but the monkey was nowhere to be seen.

"Phil?" he said, stepping toward the burning ruins, the dust now all around them.

Eisenstone grabbed his shoulder, holding him back. "Don't go any closer."

"Phil!" Tim yelled. "Where is he?"

Dee covered her mouth, looking on. The professor too seemed worried as seconds passed and the monkey still didn't emerge.

The sound of sirens drew nearer. At the front of the house, through the broken gate, a fire engine and three police cars arrived. Their lights flickered blue, but their noise grew silent as Tim stared at what was left of Crowfield House.

The building buckled and collapsed farther as flames spiraled. A thick mass of black smoke flowed up, speckled and glowing, leaving a long shadow over the gardens. On top of the hill, it would be seen from miles away, filling the sky.

Tim sat on the ground, and his chin began to tremble. Phil was in there somewhere. Warm tears fell from his cheeks.

Blinking, Tim thought he saw a shape on the grass. It moved, and moved some more. Then a tiny monkey emerged, limping toward them. Tim stood, ran, and skidded on his knees. The monkey's fur was blackened and his paw injured, but he was alive.

"Phil!" Tim shouted as he picked him up.

Dee and Eisenstone stood over them. "Oh yes, yes, well done, little monkey," the professor said, crouching, the fire reflecting in his glasses.

"What a strange day," Dee said.

"Indeed."

"That monster tried to *kill* Clarice," Tim said. "Her own creation, the first thing she made, wanted to destroy her." They stood and watched the burning wreckage for a moment.

"I wonder," the monkey added, "what a psychiatrist would say about that."

CHAPTER 24

Tim, Dee, and Eisenstone gave what proved to be long, complex statements at the police station. The officer conducting the interviews spent a lot of time rubbing his forehead and asking them to repeat themselves. Some men in suits also arrived and quizzed them on all that had taken place at Crowfield House.

All cleaned up and back at the Dawn Star, Tim took the Imagination Box from his bag and placed the reader inside. After closing the lid, he carried the device to his closet and put it on one of the shelves, on top of some old board games. His finger ran over the large black question mark on the side, with a tap on the dot.

Smiling, he shut the closet door.

Later, he was propped up in bed, with Phil in the top drawer next to him and Elisa sitting by his side. It took hours for her to stop asking questions, which was fair enough. Tim answered them as best he could, but if it hadn't been for a talking monkey backing up his claims, she'd have found believing the entire story quite difficult.

After a long chat, Tim settled down into his pillow and, even though he was completely and utterly exhausted, his mind still buzzed with the day's events.

"Sweet dreams," Elisa said, flicking the light switch off as she left.

No more than three seconds later, and the trap against the vent hissed quietly as it was edged out a little, and then slipped off onto the floor. Tim's nightmarish creation was in the room, on the carpet—covered in fresh foam, which wasn't quite as effective as he had imagined. Somehow, the creature's terrifically awful existence had slipped his mind.

He sat bolt upright in bed, staring at what he thought he had just heard. A shadow, something moving toward him.

"Elisa," he finally screamed. "Elisa!"

The door swung open, and the light flashed on. She stormed fearlessly toward the monster, grabbed it by one of its legs, and held it up at arm's length. It wiggled, writhed, and snapped at her.

"Did you make this?" she asked, frowning and raising the corner of her top lip.

"Yes, by accident," Tim replied.

"It's a funny thing, isn't it?" She lifted it higher to get a good look at its body. It snarled and hissed. "What does it even do?"

Tim considered this. Now that he thought about it, he didn't know what the beast was going to do when it caught him. Maybe that was why it had never actually attacked, just followed him around. It wasn't the feeling of being hurt that frightened him in the nightmare, nor being eaten or anything like that—it was just being chased, just being . . . *alone.* Seeing Elisa hold it in such a casual way made the creature seem somehow ridiculous.

"Shall I get rid of it?" she asked.

"Yes, please."

"Maybe I'll take it to the zoo in the morning. See what they think."

"Good idea."

"Right," she said, holding the weighty creature far from herself as it had one last screech. "Good night again."

And, just like that, Elisa took the fear away.

Tim touched the top of his head to double-check that he wasn't wearing his hat. Finally, he lay still and felt safe. His imagination relaxed, and sleep, *real sleep,* gradually took him.

EPILOGUE

A couple of weeks later, Tim was sitting in the lobby, his hand swaying left to right as he sketched a human brain. Although he could have created this drawing instantly with the Imagination Box, there was still something satisfying about the time and effort required to do it the old-fashioned way. Sometimes the fun is in the journey, not the destination, he thought.

Donald Pinkman's time at the hotel had drawn to a close. Near the front door the consultant bid farewell to fellow staff, then finally stepped over to Tim.

"That's very good," Donald said, nodding at the sketch pad. "Well, I'm off."

"All right." Tim smiled. "See ya. Oh, and I'm sorry for accusing you of kidnapping Eisenstone."

"You did what now?"

"It was my mistake. Coincidences, eh?" It had turned out that Donald really *had* just wanted to protect the hotel's reputation.

Bewildered, Donald paused and then had one last stab at an authoritative tone. "Didn't Elisa say you shouldn't draw in the lobby—messy fingerprints on the sofa . . . ?"

"Okay," Tim said. "Bye, then."

That evening, Elisa, Chris, Tim, and Phil went to a science seminar at Glassbridge's large, grand theater. There was a series of lectures hosted by prominent professors and academics. The headline slot was Professor Eisenstone, who, according to the program, would speak about the exciting advances in "quantum nanoscience."

Eisenstone's daughter, Sarah, was there with her husband. Dee was too, wearing her polka-dot dress and the hair band Tim had made. They all sat along the same row and watched excitedly as the professor took the stage.

It was obvious he was nervous, lit brightly in front of royal-red curtains. A cube-shaped prop by his side was hidden by a purple velvet sheet.

He approached the microphone and began to speak. "There is a box," he said. "Anything you imagine will appear inside. You have one go, one chance to create *anything* you want. What would you pick?"

In broad terms he explained, thanks to some "incredible technology," that this might one day be a reality. However, he said that it was still "many years away." Dee and Tim shared a knowing glance at this—they weren't surprised by Eisenstone's decision not to share *exactly* what had happened over the past few weeks.

Nonetheless, the audience was visibly excited, especially when he revealed a mocked-up prototype.

After the seminar, the professor invited Elisa, Chris, and Tim back to his house for dinner. He was cooking at the barbecue when they arrived in the large garden, already populated by Dee and her parents.

"Ah! Yes, yes, indeed yes. My guest of honor," the professor said, pointing his cooking tongs to the sky. He took his apron off and came to greet them. "Tim, let me show you around."

As they walked away from everyone else, Tim glanced back, slightly concerned to see Chris rubbing his hands and approaching the barbecue.

"He is going to destroy dinner," Tim said. "It's as simple as that."

They headed a little farther past the flower beds. Eisenstone was in a jubilant mood, still animated by the presentation. "I think it went well, yes, indeed."

"People seemed interested," Tim said.

"It's . . . it's been a rocky road. How have you been since . . . ?"

Tim knew what he meant. "It was weird having someone else's thoughts in my brain. Odd dreams and stuff, but, you know, I'll live." He looked at his feet, nervous to ask about what he'd seen. "What happened . . . that day . . . in the lab, with you and Whitelock . . . It was . . ."

The professor seemed to know the topic was about to come up—he put on a brave face to explain. "Yes. Indeed," he said. "Now you know. . . . You see, well, some of the earlier readers were a little . . . dodgy. The Imagination Box has been an idea for a long time, but it's only recently become what you might call stable. Back then, it was really new ground. Oh yes, we had no real idea what we were doing. The old readers used radiation, like an X-ray of the brain. After that day, after that failed test, Whitelock, well, he was never the same again."

"I felt that."

"Yes. He was always keen to experiment on himself. There was always something about him, a part of his mind that made him *obsessed* with progress. But progress at *any cost*. It's quite hard to understand, really."

"No it isn't. I get it," Tim said. "He believed scientific advancement was more important than anything else."

Eisenstone slowed a little, looking warily at Tim. "That's exactly it," he said. "You sound just like him.

Anyway, we drifted apart after that failed test. I assumed he blamed me for what happened, for the damage to his mind. I know I've always blamed myself."

"It's not your fault," Tim said. "He wanted to do it. I saw the memory. He was happy to risk anything to make it work. And later Clarice just took advantage of him. He was a victim of her, and of himself—*you* have no reason to feel guilty."

Eisenstone seemed lightened, as though he'd been waiting years to hear those words. "Thank you."

Tim listened to the birds chirping above them, thinking of all that had happened at Crowfield House. Stephen and Kane had been arrested, and Whitelock had, once again, gone missing. Of course, Tim had not been surprised to hear that there was absolutely no trace of Clarice.

They rounded a low bush and headed toward the house. Before they made it back to the table, the professor stopped.

"I was wrong about the box," Eisenstone said, almost to himself. "I told you it could only make concrete things. It just isn't that simple. Indeed. We've seen hate and obsession; we've seen loneliness and fear." He glanced at Tim's top pocket. "And we've seen loyalty and love. We scientists occasionally get carried away—indeed, we sometimes think we know more than we do. The Imagination Box is no different. It's more than a tool; it's more than a toy; it is a bridge, a bridge between our minds and the physical world. We've barely scratched the surface."

Later on, Tim, Dee, and Phil sat together at the back of the lawn near the flowers and tomato plants. Through the trees the orange light painted leopard-print patterns as they idly chatted the evening away.

Tim looked back at the adults, sitting around the table, sipping wine and laughing. He saw Eisenstone pull his silver watch from his pocket to check the time, as Chris cut up a sausage on a plate.

Phil, who had been well behaved most of the day, hidden in Tim's pocket, was now on the ground looking for a clover with four leaves.

"So what, precisely, is it that makes them lucky?" the monkey asked, wading amid the rich turf that was, for him, waist high.

"It's just superstition," Tim explained. "Because they are rare, unique."

The air between them swirled now with the faint smells of summer: barbecue smoke, fresh pollen, and the cool grass beneath.

"At any rate, I think some good fortune would be quite desirable," the monkey said. "Perhaps if my search is unsuccessful, which seems terribly probable, you could make me one?"

"Sure," Tim said. "If that's what you really want."

Dee picked up a dandelion and blew gently into the fluffed top. "It's a strange thing to consider," she said, squinting through the dancing seeds.

"What is?" Phil asked.

"Having *anything* you want," Dee said. "You could see people in the audience earlier—they were all wondering what it'd be. What they would choose. It's an interesting question."

Right then Tim caught Elisa's eye, and she gave him a comforting smile. "Yeah, it is," he whispered.

Glancing around at everyone in the garden—warm and hazy in the last of the day's sun—Tim realized that his answer was relatively simple.

He couldn't imagine needing anything else.

ABOUT THE AUTHOR

MARTYN FORD is a journalist from Hampshire, England, where he writes for the *Bordon Herald*. His first book, *It Happened to Me,* is a collection of shocking true stories. *The Imagination Box* is his first story for young readers. Visit Martyn at martyn-ford.com.